DRAMA!

Entrances and Exits

Paul Ruditis

Simon Pulse
NEW YORK LONDON TORONTO SYDNEY

SIMON PULSE

An imprint of Simon & Schuster Children's Publishing Division

1230 Avenue of the Americas, New York, NY 10020

Copyright © 2008 by Paul Ruditis

All rights reserved, including the right of reproduction in whole or in part in any form.

SIMON PULSE and colophon are registered trademarks of Simon & Schuster, Inc.

Designed by Mike Rosamilia

The text of this book was set in Weiss.

Manufactured in the United States of America

First Simon Pulse edition August 2008

2 4 6 8 10 9 7 5 3 1

Library of Congress Control Number 2008924473

ISBN-13: 978-1-4169-5906-9

ISBN-10: 1-4169-5906-8

☆ For the Northeast High School Brat Pack ☆
We were so high school . . . except not.

Acknowledgments

To the editors extraordinaire at Simon Pulse who put a little bit of themselves in DRAMA!: Lisa Clancy, Bethany Buck, Michelle Nagler, and especially the one who shared the DRAMA! with me the longest, Michael del Rosario . . .

To the artists responsible for some of my favorite covers ever: Ann Zeak, Russell Gordon, Cara Petrus, Mike Rosamilia, and Ali Smith . . .

To Jean Gaskill for (unintentional) inspiration, and to Tim, Harry, and Johnny for keeping that inspiration sane . . .

To the first people to experience the DRAMA!: Chris Van Note, Chip Carter, and Babe Root (yes, that's her name) . . .

To Phyllis Ungerleider, Christina Hahni, Lili Rossi (and Dave and Frankie), Susan Askew, Shawn Ku, and all my friends and family too numerous to list on this page . . .

And especially to the readers . . .

I thank you.

The Producers

Sam took the stage, as I'd seen her do many times before. She stepped out from the wings with a commanding presence, daring us to look away. Moving downstage center, she stopped a few feet from the edge, at home under the bright lights.

"My name is Sam Lawson," she said in a clear voice. "And I'll be performing the part of Felicia from Hope Rivera's play, *Achromantic*." Sam had chosen one of the three parts we'd selected for the girls to audition with. None of us was surprised that Felicia was the monologue that Sam had chosen. The playwright, Hope Rivera, is our other best friend.

Sam closed her eyes, taking a deep breath. It was part of her traditional preparation for an audition. Her body language shifted as she took on the character. People who didn't know her probably wouldn't have noticed it at all. But to me the transition was clearly evident. Sam's eyes blinked open. She was prepared to begin.

"NEXT!" I shouted.

"Bryan!" she screeched in response as her carefully constructed character fell apart.

I was laughing too hard to fear for my life at the moment. "Sorry. Couldn't resist." But seriously, like I needed Sam to audition for me. Like our teachers, Mr. Randall and Ms. Monroe, weren't already familiar with her talents either. We each wanted her to star in the one-act plays we were directing. The only question was who was going to get her?

"Bryan." Mr. Randall gave me a teacherly disappointed look that made me realize the tactical mistake I had just made. If I wanted to get Sam to be in my play, juvenile games like that during an audition were *so* not the way to make it happen. But in case I didn't get the message on my own, he had to give me the lecture. "I realize you and Sam are friends, but I would expect you to behave in a more professional manner during an audition. I only agreed to allow you to direct because I thought you were mature enough to handle it. Please do not make me regret this decision."

Wow. He didn't use a single contraction there. He must've been upset.

I suspected that it wasn't a good idea to point out that he'd mainly agreed to allow me to direct because the playwright— namely Hope—had told him that she wanted it to happen. Mr. Randall was more afraid of upsetting Hope than anything. Not that Hope is the real problem, mind you. Oh, she can be downright frightening when she's mad. Seriously. You don't want to see her angry. But the real intimidation comes from the power she wields in having a father who is a big-time lawyer to the stars. Hope would never take advantage of our teacher's fear, like so many other students at our school do on regular occasion, but Mr. Randall has worked in Malibu long enough that he knows to avoid the risk by keeping the students happy. And keeping Hope happy meant making me the director. Though I like to believe that part of the reason I got the job was based on merit.

"My apologies," I said with my best attempt at a professional demeanor. "Ms. Lawson, you may proceed."

Sam squinted in my direction. I could tell she was weighing the risks of being unprofessional herself and laying into me for interrupting her audition. With her talent she could get away with almost anything. But she didn't. She closed those squinting eyes again, took another deep breath, and launched into the monologue I could now recite by heart. And I was usually lousy at memorizing dialogue.

My familiarity with the text had nothing to do with having heard it a half dozen times already during the auditions— though that certainly didn't hurt. Since Hope gave me a copy of her play back on the first day of school, I'd probably read it a hundred times. No lie. I may be prone to exaggeration from time to time, but not in this case. Recent behavior aside, I was taking this whole directing thing very seriously. Not because I was the first student in Orion Academy history to direct a play in the Fall One-Act Festival. Not because I was hoping to redeem myself after learning that some people thought I wasn't the best actor in the world. And certainly not because I felt I had anything to prove to some of my more obnoxious classmates.

No, it was mainly because if I screwed up Hope's play, she'd *kill* me.

Fear is a handy motivator.

The full significance of this event was not lost on me, though. Hope was also the first student ever to have a play produced in the showcase. It used to be that the one-acts were directed by Mr. Randall, Ms. Monroe, and a celebrity guest. The thing is, celebrity guests hadn't worked out all that well in recent history. The faculty had been considering dropping that element of the festival when Hope came along with her first stab at a short play. I'm told that once Mr. Randall read it, he couldn't say no. And not because Hope had threatened him or anything. Her play, *Achromantic*, was just that good.

Now, you might think I'm biased, with Hope being one of my best friends and all. And I am. I freely admit that. But *every* girl who auditioned for the festival was allowed to choose a monologue from one of the three plays we were putting on for the show. And so far *every* girl had chosen to read Hope's. Even our old archnemesis, Holly Mayflower.

You can't get much more of a recommendation than that, can you?

Although part of me would like to believe they were also excited about the possibility of working with me as a director. You know, because any serious actress would prefer to work with an amateur who doesn't know what the heck he's doing as opposed to two professional educators with years of directorial experience under their belts . . . who also could get you out of class for additional rehearsal time if necessary.

"Thank you, Sam," Mr. Randall said, pulling me out of my wandering thoughts. As a director—and a friend—I should have paid more attention to her audition, but I had a lot on my mind. In addition to the casting there was the actual directing of the play itself. Then there was the design of the play, the costumes, and all that. Surely I was going to have help with those things, but I was also going to have to be the final word on everything. This being a high school production, we didn't have a huge staff at our disposal. We were more like producer-directors, truth be told. This was particularly exciting because I could then think of myself as a producer-director-photographer, which raised me to a double hyphenate for the first time in my life.

See, hyphens are how we judge success in the L.A. area. The more hyphens in your title, the more successful you are. Me? I've made it into a bit of a game. It isn't much of a fun game considering I can never manage to come up with a good hyphenated title for myself, but I'm working on it. And I admit, the "photographer" part of me is more a hobby than a lifestyle. But this "producer" thing could work. Granted, I didn't have any money invested in the Fall One-Act Festival. Mr. Randall was actually the one who would make all the final decisions about the big stuff. Even Headmaster Collins will have the ultimate say in things like how we cover the budget.

People will probably be checking over my shoulder every step of the way.

Okay. Fine. Back to director-photographer.

Even though I wasn't feeling much like a real director yet.

I shot Sam a smile as I came back to reality while she left the stage. No doubt she was getting a lead part. I only hoped it would be in my play.

"Hope, no!" our intrepid stage manager yelled from the stage door. Poor Jimmy Wilkey didn't have a chance as Hope barreled past him and onto the stage.

"Just one thing. Only going to be a moment," she said as she crossed the stage, ignoring Jimmy and aiming directly for me.

"Hope, this is a closed audition," Mr. Randall reminded her for the umpteenth time. "That means no other students. And especially no playwrights."

"But I want to make sure that Bryan—"

"He does," Mr. Randall said. "Whatever it is you want to make sure of, he knows it, he's done it, or he intends to do it. You chose him to be your director. Now you have to trust him to do his job."

For some reason my mind continued the line as ". . . and suffer the consequences."

"But—"

"Thank you, Hope," Mr. Randall said. "Jimmy, please escort our playwright out of the audition."

"Ummmm."

Yeah. I couldn't blame him for fearing the death glare.

"Hope," I called to her. "Don't kill him for doing his job."

"Fine," she said, storming off. And I was the one getting in trouble for behaving in an unprofessional manner earlier?

"Next!" Jimmy called into the hall as he exited with Hope following her brief cameo.

Suddenly it became clear to me why Hope had interrupted. Belinda, one of Hope's evil stepsisters was next in line. Mind you, it was the less evil of the stepsisters, but that was only a matter of degrees. Hope probably had come out to warn me not to bother paying any attention since I wouldn't be casting her.

While it was no surprise that Belinda's leader, Holly Mayflower, would audition for the Fall One-Act Festival, Belinda was new to this whole acting thing and an unknown commodity. Her sister, Alexis, had proven she had no acting chops whatsoever, so I was pretty sure she wouldn't be setting foot onstage. Still, Hope should have known me well enough to trust that I would never cast any member of that particular evil trio in her play.

"My name is Belinda Connors," she said as her skinny little legs took her center stage. "And I'll be performing a mono- logue from *Achromantic*."

Great. I couldn't figure out what she was pulling by coming in to audition for Hope's play, but it didn't matter. The mono- logue selection was just so the actors could indicate what play they preferred. Us directors were free to ignore their feelings entirely and cast them in any of the three plays. Since I wasn't going to be casting her in mine, I started silently working on my argument to get Mr. Randall and Ms. Monroe to let me have Sam for my play. I wanted Jason MacMillan to play the male lead. Still wasn't sure about the other female part, but there were several contenders that would be . . . acceptable.

A discreet cough from the stage pulled me back into the moment. I thought Belinda was clearing her throat, but that didn't explain the change that had come over her. Always the shyest of the evil trio, Belinda looked downright timid onstage. Had stage fright affected her that dramatically? I figured I should pay attention since the story of her tragic collapse during the audition would provide hours of entertainment for me, Sam, and especially Hope.

"Excuse me," she said meekly. "I'm not sure what to do." I was going to ask if she needed something explained to her . . . slowly . . . with small words . . . but then I realized she wasn't confused. She was doing a different monologue from the play.

I'd chosen the part of Felicia as the audition piece. It was the stronger of the female roles and had the biggest emotional arc in it. Felicia is the "other woman" in a love triangle, struggling with her feelings for a man she should not love. Every girl so far had played by the rules and chosen that monologue. Leave it to Belinda to go and pick the other female character in the play. I would have stopped everything to say something about it, but Belinda was doing well enough that I decided to let her continue.

Belinda went through the monologue, finding something interesting in every vulnerable beat. I caught myself leaning on the back of the chair in front of me, utterly absorbed by her performance. Though the Rachel character was in less of the play than the other two, she was the most nuanced of the roles. While Sam was going to have a challenge bringing her character down to keep the audience from hating her for stealing Rachel's man, whoever I picked to play Rachel was going to face the daunting task of elevating her character above being a doormat. It was all there in Hope's script. I just wasn't sure that any girl at our school could pull it off.

"Um . . . is that all?" Belinda asked. I'd been so wrapped up in her performance that I didn't even realize she was done until after about ten seconds of awkward silence while we three directors stared at her in amazement.

"Yes," Mr. Randall said, pulling his tongue up off the floor, where it lay next to mine. (Okay, *that's* a disgusting visual.) "Thank you, Belle."

As she walked back to the stage door, I shared a confused look with my teachers. They were as shocked as I was. Belinda had never shown anywhere near that level of performance before. Heck, before the Summer Theatrical Program a few months back, she'd never even shown any interest in performing. I'd say she was a natural talent, but I wasn't sure where that talent came from. Surely not from her mom, the washed-up eighties pop-culture cult sensation, Kara Bow. These things probably skip a generation.

The remaining auditions were good, if uneventful. We had a number of fine actors and actresses in our school. Of those I found a couple of girls who could play the part of Rachel well enough. But no one really hit it for me. Well, no one I could cast in the part and still expect to live.

While Mr. Randall went out into the hall to thank everyone for their auditions and Ms. Monroe ran out the back of the auditorium to throw up (more on that later), I mentally prepared for the coming battle over Sam and Jason. The role of Rachel could pretty much go to anyone, since no one—other than Belinda—had that wow factor. Seeing how Belinda wasn't an option, I had to concentrate on the fight for the actors I wanted. Maybe I could suggest Belinda to my teachers if either of them wanted Sam.

Mr. Randall and Ms. Monroe might still be so awestruck by Belinda that they wouldn't notice I got the way better end of the deal.

"A nice batch of auditions," Mr. Randall said once he and Ms. Monroe returned from their errands. "What did you think, Bryan?"

"It was weird being on the other side of things," I said. "Never been in the inner circle before."

"That sounds so much more clandestine than it really is," Ms. Monroe said.

"So what now?" I asked. "Do we have a battle royal to see who gets what actors? 'Cause I'm not so sure I can take Ms. Monroe. Even in her condition."

"Nothing so exciting," Mr. Randall said. "Who would you like to cast in your play?"

"Well," I said, opening up negotiations. "There were several people I would consider for the roles. Not that I would be presumptuous enough to expect that they would be available."

My teachers shared a look that could only be described as "amused."

"Bryan," Mr. Randall said. "Just tell us you want Sam and we can start there. Ms. Monroe and I have already agreed that you should have the first choice of actors since you're the student."

"Really?" I asked, feeling kind of let down. I was anticipating a negotiation on par with the great debates of history. Or at least something like the catty bickering they have on *The View*. "You sure?"

"Positive," Ms. Monroe said.

"Okay," I said. "Then I'd like Sam and Jason for the parts of Felicia and Mackenzie."

"We assumed," Mr. Randall said, placing a pair of check marks on his audition sheet. "But before we finalize that, I want to make sure you're going to be okay with directing one of your best friends."

"I'm looking forward to it," I said, imagining all the fun things I was going to make Sam do. I guess there was something about the malevolent gleam in my eye that earned me a warning glare from both my teachers. "What?" I asked innocently.

"And the third part?" Ms. Monroe asked. "The role of Rachel?"

This was the hard one. There were a couple classmates I could cast. What it ultimately came down to was the one who I figured would be most fun to work with. Certainly, no one had impressed me enough to stand out. "Tasha?" I said with uncertainty.

My teachers frowned at each other in a rather telling way. I swear some teachers have this, like, silent language perfected.

"Tasha's a fine actress," Mr. Randall said.

"And she'll do well in the part," Ms. Monroe added.

It was like they were tag-teaming me. I was just waiting for the—

"But," Mr. Randall supplied, "how did you feel about Belle's audition?"

"Belinda?" I asked. "She was okay."

"Bryan, it would be a real shame to let a good actress go because of personal animosities," he said.

"I don't have any animosity toward Belinda," I said. "She's never done anything to me." You know . . . *directly*.

Mr. Randall continued to make his case. "I know that Hope doesn't have the closest relationship with her sisters—"

"*Step*sisters," I corrected in a rather unhelpful manner.

His face got all screwed up in frustration, but he continued, "As the director, it is your responsibility to put up the best show possible. I think you know that Belle would be wonderful in the role, if her audition is any indication."

Don't you hate it when people tell you what you should know?

"But isn't it also the director's responsibility"—I could play this game too—"to create an environment that allows his production to flow as smoothly as possible?"

There was a pause while my teachers reconsidered their

approach. I wasn't prepared with the one they came up with, as it was fairly unusual for the Orion Academy staff to be, you know, *honest*. "Okay, seriously," Mr. Randall said. "We took a big risk allowing one student to write a play for the festival and another student to direct it. You're the most observant student I've ever met." What a nice way to call me nosey. "You can imagine the phone calls we got from parents who were upset that we picked you two over their own children. We dealt with those calls because we have faith in you and in Hope. But if you can't even cast the play without letting childish fights get in the way, then I'm not so sure we made the right decision."

Ouch.

I mean, really . . .

Ouch.

Stage Door

I took as much time as humanly possible packing up my stuff. Heck, I even took some *inhumanly* possible time too. Mr. Randall had written out the cast list for all three one-act plays and handed it to our fearless stage manager, Jimmy, for him to type up and post first thing the next day. I'd been forbidden to tell anyone who was on it. I was especially forbidden to tell who was *not* on it. I wasn't even allowed to let Hope know, even though she had a stake in the production. That's the way it's done. The cast list goes up the morning after auditions so the students have the rest of the school day to calm down before going home and complaining to their parents about their parts, or lack thereof. Personally, I've always suspected that the main reason we're not allowed to have cell phones on campus is to avoid immediate calls home whenever a teacher does something a student doesn't like. The teachers get enough calls from parental units as it is.

But I remind you, I was the first student—aside from Jimmy—to know who was cast before the list went up. Everyone knows not to pester Jimmy. You see, Jimmy's a little high-strung. One day he's going to snap. Not in some horrific "film at eleven" sort of way. It will probably present itself in more of a subtly embarrassing manner, like his wetting himself in the middle of the hallway. No one wants to be around when that happens. So we all leave him alone at times like these. It's safer. And dryer.

Me? Everyone knows I can't keep a secret. Well, there was one. But just because I didn't tell that secret doesn't mean everyone didn't know anyway. You know? Still, when there's information to be gleaned, I'm usually a reliable source. Particularly for my friends.

It was those friends I was dreading encountering as I checked the seats to make sure I wasn't forgetting anything. Anything at all. Anything that would add another few precious seconds before I had to follow my teachers out of the safety of the auditorium.

Got my books?

In my bag.

Got my fedora?

On my head.

Got my classic-style Five Time Zone automatic watch from Jacob the Jeweler?

I don't actually own one of those, but I checked for it anyway. Never know when a watch like that might pop up unexpectedly. Kind of always wanted a Five Time Zone watch.

Never can tell when someone might ask you for the time in Malibu, New York, Paris, Tokyo, and Zimbabwe all at once. But since I didn't own such a watch and one wasn't to be found, I figured I'd stalled as much as I could.

Mr. Randall and Ms. Monroe had already left, paving the way for me to go. If I stayed alone in the theater any longer, people were going to talk. I didn't know what they'd say about me spending so much time by myself in the school auditorium, but I had faith they could come up with some good rumors. This is Orion Academy after all.

And so I slung my bag over my shoulder and ditched out the main doors at the back of the Saundra Hall Auditorium (aka Hall Hall), figuring that everyone was still hanging out behind the stage door.

I figured wrong.

A chorus of "Bryan's" greeted me as I stepped out into the foyer. Various seniors, juniors, sophomores, and freshmen were clamoring for my attention. Never in my life have I been this popular. What I noticed most, however, was the lack of my closest friends in the crowd. Straining over the heads of those smaller than me—I am kind of on the tall side—I did see Sam over by the school waterfall. She was talking to Tasha Valentine, barely noticing I was there.

"First thing tomorrow morning," I said to the gathered masses, exactly as Mr. Randall had instructed me to do. "The cast list comes up first thing tomorrow morning."

"But, Bryan—" Madison Wu said.

"Tomorrow morning," I insisted, figuring if I stuck to the

same few words, there'd be less of a chance I'd slip and say something wrong. Like telling Madison she was cast in Ms. Monroe's play and congratulating her for being the only junior to get a leading role.

There was some grumbling, but everyone let me pass. While they did clear a path, they weren't quite dispersing as I'd hoped. I guess they suspected that I would give my best friend more intel, so they were all sticking around to eavesdrop. Can't say I blame them. I'd have done the same in their situation.

"Bryan," said a male voice behind me.

"Tomorrow morning," I said without turning.

Then I felt a hand on my shoulder. "Hold on," he said, giving me a gentle squeeze. "I want to ask you something."

I turned to find Gary McNulty, better known as Monkey Boy for his scene-stealing turn in our show-stealing production of *The Wizard of Oz* the previous spring. (*Aside:* I call it "show-stealing" because somebody literally tried to steal the show.)

"Gary," I said, trying to head him off. "Seriously. You should know . . ." I paused, realizing something I hadn't noticed before. "You didn't audition. Why didn't you audition?" Gary is one of the best actors in the junior class. Sure, he leans more toward comedy where the Fall One-Act Festival veers more toward drama, but it wasn't like him to pass up a chance to perform. Unlike me, he tends to enjoy the spotlight.

"The good parts always go to the seniors in the Fall Fest,"

he said, which was as true this year as always. Like I'd already mentioned, Gary's best friend, Madison, was the only junior to get a primo part.

"Yeah, but I've seen you make the most of a simple walk through a scene," I replied. As the lead flying monkey in *Wizard* he threw in a death-defying (and nearly concussion-inducing) stage leap during what should have been a simple exit.

"I kind of had something different in mind," he said rather shyly. Which was odd. I mean, you don't get a nickname like Monkey Boy for being timid.

"Uh-huh?" I said, wondering where this was going.

"So, it's like," he said, "you know, this acting thing may not work out. 'Cause like what are the odds?" *Better for him than for most*, I thought. *Like me.* "I figure it doesn't hurt to learn about different jobs in the theater."

"I think you're going to do fine with the acting," I told him. Aside from the innate talent, Gary also possessed cute boyish good looks that were so popular with casting agents in these days of the Zac Efron effect. Brown curly hair, silver-framed glasses, and a constant innocent expression all pretty much guaranteed Gary could be cast tomorrow in the next Disney movie musical or any of the dramas on the CW.

"Still," he insisted. "I was wondering. Do you have a stage manager?"

The question caught me by surprise. I wasn't sure what to say. I'd been so focused on my cast, I hadn't really thought about technical support. "I think Jimmy's going to be stage manager for all three of us."

"Well, sure," he said. "I figured Jimmy'd be running the show. But I mean someone to help out at rehearsals and stuff. Jimmy can't be there for you, Mr. Randall, and Ms. Monroe all at the same time."

I wasn't so sure about that. If anyone could manage to be in three different places at once, it was Jimmy Wilkey. He ensures that by keeping himself constantly fueled by Starbucks Frappuccinos. Still, Gary's idea did have merit. I could probably use the help. And he was always fun to have around. "I guess," I said. "Let me talk to Mr. Randall."

"Sure!" he said. All his shyness was gone. "Sounds good. You just tell me when you know. Great. That's great!" Then it's possible he realized he was being a little overeager, because he quickly added, "We can talk about compensation, the benefits package, and the size of my office once you get clearance for the job. Oh, and I'm going to need the first week off for personal reasons. You understand, of course?"

"Of course," I replied.

"Seriously, though," he said. "Thanks. This is going to be fun." I couldn't say anything about the fun aspect. I was more focused on my crippling fear of failure that could permeate every facet of our working relationship, but I didn't want to ruin his day by causing him to worry about his director. Smiling, Gary went back into the crowd, searching for his best friend, while I continued toward mine.

"Hey," I said when I reached Sam. She was now alone at the waterfall. Tasha wasn't the type to pump anyone for information, so she probably left before the temptation got the better of her. "What's a nice girl like you doing in a place like this?"

"I was waitin' here, hopin' some kind gentleman would come along and take pity on a poor lonely gal," Sam said in a pitch-perfect Southern accent, which stopped very suddenly. *"And take me to work, like you promised."*

Oh yeah.

"Conveniently, I happen to be heading in just that direction," I said. We were expecting a late delivery at my mom's new store, Kaye 9: Li'l Beaches. Modeled after the original spot for designer doggie duds, Kaye 9 on Melrose Ave, the Malibu location was even more popular than the flagship boutique. Sam and I had agreed to help inventory the items since we wouldn't be finishing up at school until late, and Mom didn't want to have to pay anyone else to come in for a full shift. Seeing how I'm the second assistant manager, it wasn't so much a favor as part of my job.

As Sam and I headed out of school, I braced myself for the inevitable.

"You think the new glow-in-the-dark chew toys will be coming in today?"

Okay, that wasn't the inevitable I'd been bracing myself for.

"Beats me," I said. "The distributor is notoriously late with the shipments. Blaine always wants to cancel our order, but the Malibu wives love their products. Especially now that it's getting dark earlier."

"I know," Sam replied. "I started a waiting list over the weekend."

I couldn't believe we were actually talking about the inventory of my mom's store when Sam should have been trying to wheedle information out of me on the casting. Not that I was going to tell her anything, but we had to go through the motions at the very least.

"What are the odds Blaine will let me pick up a couple extra hours this Saturday?" Sam asked. "I could use some extra cash."

"I don't see why not," I replied. Blaine, my mom's best friend and business partner, loves Sam so much that he pretends he enjoys working with her more than me. At least, I *think* it's pretend.

"We've been getting busier now that people know we're in town," I said. Add to that all the doggie Halloween costumes my mom had been designing for her clientele and it was going to be a very happy holiday season in the Stark household. Might as well share the wealth with Sam.

But back to the main plot.

"Didn't Hope stick around?" I asked as we left the building, expecting to be jumped at any moment by a rogue author in search of six—well, *three*—characters. (*Aside:* That's a joke. See, there's a play called *Six Characters in Search of an Author*, and I was making a . . . never mind. If I have to explain it, it's not funny.) "I thought her face would be the first one I saw when I got out of auditions."

"It would've," Sam said with a shrug. "But Mr. Randall told her to go home. He didn't want her attacking you to find out who you cast in her play."

"Oh." I nodded as if it made perfect sense. It did, really. But

I wasn't sure why Sam wasn't attacking me all the same. "There were some very good auditions," I added.

"I'm glad," Sam said. "You want to grab dinner after work, or should I call Mom and tell her to wait for me?"

"Whatever," I said. My mind was too confused to decide on dinner. Sam usually freaked out after an audition and couldn't shut up about it until the cast list went up the next day. I'd be getting calls from her on my cell phone all night long, second-guessing everything she did and debating—with herself—if she gave a good enough audition for a lead. Now I couldn't even get her to talk about the audition? Not that I was supposed to be talking about it, but still!

Not a word was said about the Fall One-Act Festival as we walked all the way out of school and to my car, Electra, at the far end of the parking lot.

Once we were inside, I gave the subject another shot. I was worried that the reason Sam didn't want to talk about it was because she didn't want me to cast her in the play I was directing. I mean, we'd been talking all along about how she wanted to be in the play Hope wrote. But to work with me? We'd never discussed that part of it. Maybe she wasn't interested. As her director I'd sort of be her boss. And, okay, I was kind of her boss at the store, because I was second assistant manager and all, but that was different. I knew better than to tell her what to do at work. I usually left that kind of thing to Mom or Blaine. As Sam's director it would be my duty to tell her what I needed her to do. A duty that I couldn't pass off to someone else.

"Sure did turn out to be a nice day," Sam said.

"I have to tell you about auditions!" I finally burst, clutching tightly to Electra's steering wheel. I mean *seriously*? We were going to talk about the weather?

"Didn't see *that* coming" was Sam's calm reply.

I paused. "If you're going to be that way about it, I'll just keep it to myself."

"Mm-hmm," she said, turning away from me to gaze out the window.

"Okay. Fine!" I said. "I'll tell you!"

Now she actually looked at me. *There* was the face of nervous anticipation that I'd come to know and adore following an audition. No matter how many people constantly tell Sam that she's a great actress, I don't think she ever totally believes them. It's like every time she goes out for a role at our school, she genuinely believes she doesn't have a chance of getting it.

Naturally, I had to have some fun with her first.

"I cast Jason as Mackenzie," I said excitedly.

Her eyes got that threatening look. "Good choice," she said through clenched teeth. "And for the girls?"

"It was a difficult decision," I said, stalling. "I mean, Holly did give a good audition." I knew I was risking my life by dropping the name of her nemesis, but . . . Sam started it!

Her fingers were tapping on the dashboard to an annoyed beat.

"Okay, fine," I said, giving in *way* too easily. "You're Felicia!"

"Yes!" she said, giving a fist pump in the air. "Felicia is such a great part. Hope totally understands how to write for women."

"And you're excited to work with your best friend as your director," I reminded her.

"Obviously," she said, though I could swear there was some hesitation in her voice. Then again, her words were being filtered through my own doubt in myself.

"And Rachel?" she asked.

Insert heavy sigh here.

"That's not good," she said in response to my reaction. "Tell me you didn't cast Holly."

"In a supporting role?" I laughed. "Yeah. Like that would happen. No. Holly's going to be in Mr. Randall's play."

"God help Mr. Randall," Sam added as we both threw in a glance to the heavens, which could have been construed—by some—as more of an eye roll. "So what's with the hesitation? Didn't you get who you wanted?"

"Well, that's one of those yes-and-no answers," I said. "I got the person who would be best for the part, but I can't say that I got the person I wanted. Or, more specifically, I got a person I *know* Hope wouldn't want."

I paused to let Sam go over in her mind the group of people who auditioned. Even though Orion Academy did have a large talent pool to choose from, it didn't take all that long for Sam to make the connection. "No!" was all she needed to say.

I nodded.

"Belinda?"

"She gave the best audition," I said. "By far. This may be the first time she ever tried out for a show, but you should have seen her."

"She did have a good monologue in the summer program," Sam said, remembering back to the theater workshop we had at the start of last summer. "It could be worse. You could have cast Alexis." Sam invoked the name of the way wickeder of Hope's stepsisters.

"That's true!" I said, grasping on to what little comfort I could find. Not that Alexis had auditioned. "Belinda is not nearly as evil as Alexis. Hope will have to understand that I'm only doing what's best for her play. Right?"

"Because Hope is, first and foremost, a calm and rational individual," Sam agreed.

The laughter following that comment didn't come close to making me feel better.

Hellzapoppin'

"WHAT THE HELL!"

Oh good, the cast list is up.

"BRYAN!"

And yes, Hope has seen it.

But the big question was had she seen *me*?

I got my answer as soon as I turned down the hall leading away from my locker.

"Hold it!" she said as she caught up with me, moving faster than I'd seen her move in her entire life. She practically threw me into the nearest empty classroom and blocked the door.

Clearly, Hope had had no idea what the day ahead was going to be like when she got ready for school in the morning. Hope's self-titled style of dress, Goth-Ick, can usually express her mood by the severity of her almost all-black outfit and by her choice of one splash of color. Today she was in a pair of black overalls with a black T-shirt and a playful red-checkered bandana tied around her neck. Even her colored contacts were a matching playful red, though her eyes were darkening as she stood inches from me.

"I . . . how . . . why . . . ," she said before giving up. "There are no words."

If only she had meant that.

"Belinda!" she yelled, finding more words from the vast storehouse of her mind. "Belinda? Seriously? Of all the girls in the entire drama department . . . in the entire *school* . . . there wasn't one, ONE! other you could put in that role?"

Stupidly, I went for humor. "I could, but Alexis didn't audition."

My children's children will feel the pain from the death glare that she shot me at that moment.

"I will give you five minutes to call home and tell your mom good-bye," Hope said.

"My mom's at work," I said. Clearly I hadn't learned my lesson about the use of humor in this situation. If Hope had been wearing long sleeves, she would have been rolling them up.

I'd spent much of the night before rehearsing how I would respond to her. But being in the moment, under her intense gaze, it all went right out of my head. Instead of defense I went with my old standby: blame someone else. "Mr. Randall made me do it!" Which was actually kind of true. "He was the one who said that Belinda was the best choice for the role. Ms. Monroe too." At the moment, it was everyone for himself—namely me. "They wouldn't let me cast anyone else. They forced me to do it."

"*That* is your defense?" she asked.

Actually, my defense was that Belinda really was the best one for the part. She gave the best audition. She had the most potential. Take the personal animosities out of the equation and casting Belinda would be a no-brainer for any director. But that's not what Hope wanted to hear.

"How could you do this?" she asked in a calmly sad tone that was way scarier than the anger. "You know how much this play means to me. You know how much I hate those girls. Belinda is going to find some way to ruin this play. And if she does . . ."

It was a vulnerable side to Hope that few people ever see. Underneath the bravado she was as much an emotionally delicate flower as, well, *me*. She only let her closest friends witness this part of her. And only for brief glimpses.

"You need to undo this," she said threateningly.

Glimpse over.

"I can't," I replied. "The list is up. There's no way I can give the part to someone else. Mr. Randall would never let it happen. Not unless Belinda screws up during rehearsal."

"You better pray she does," Hope said. "Because if my play goes up with her on the stage, I will never forgive you." With that she stormed out of the room, leaving fear in her wake.

I peeked out the door of the classroom and watched as she continued down the hall, scaring anyone who dared to greet her. All in all, it wasn't as bad as I'd expected. I still had all my limbs and most of my emotional stability intact. Considering the worst was over, I figured I might as well swing by the callboard and see what everyone else's reactions were to the cast list. I was kind of looking forward to having Jason come up to me and call me "director." And seeing how happy everyone was about getting into the other plays would be cool too.

The reaction that was waiting for me was not entirely what I'd expected.

A sea of depressed—mostly female—faces turned as I entered the area by the call-board. The odd part was that many of those females had gotten some pretty good parts in the other one-acts. Mine was the only play with three parts. Mr. Randall's and Ms. Monroe's both had substantial casts with pretty good roles. I'd expected at least one cheery face in the group. But nothing.

"Hey, Bryan," Gary McNulty said after he pushed his way through the crowd. "You talk to Mr. Randall yet about me stage managing for you?"

"I just got here," I said in a somewhat preoccupied manner. "What's going on?"

"What?" he asked as he looked back to the zombie girls. All of them were glaring at me with disdain. Tasha in particular looked rather sullen, but then again, Tasha had a tendency toward sullenness. "Oh. I think they all wanted to be in your play."

"Really? Didn't know I was that popular."

"Um," Gary said hesitantly. "Probably has more to do with how good Hope's play is, but they could be excited about working with you too. I mean—"

"That's okay," I said. "I get it." I was still searching for a happy face. You'd think Sam would have at least stopped by to *act* surprised about being cast. Last thing I needed was her showing up like she knew she'd gotten the part. Which she did. But still, people at our school tend to search out scandal. She usually knows better than that.

"Where's Jason?" I asked, regarding my other cast member.

"Out sick," Gary replied. "He called me to see if he got cast." Gary must have caught my reaction because he quickly added, "He sounded really excited about it."

"That's good," I said, walking away from the group. It was almost time for homeroom. Clearly there was no reason for me to hang around, since the excitement of casting my first play was kind of falling flat.

A high-pitched squeal of joy cut through the misery. I turned back to see that my third cast member, Belinda, was the generator of the noise. She was hugging her best friend and tormentor, Holly, while her sister, Alexis, looked on with her usual disdain when something didn't involve her directly.

"Bryan!" Belinda called out as she pushed her way through the crowd and ran over to me. "Thank you *so much* for putting me in your play."

"It's not really—"

"This is going to be *so* great," she added. She was standing way closer to me than she'd ever been before. Usually she and her sister stand one foot behind Holly wherever they go. It's convenient that they're twins because I'm used to seeing Alexis's left side and Belinda's right side peeking out from behind Holly, so in my mind I can usually construct one person out of the two halves. Having the full Belinda up in my personal space was . . . different.

"I know I haven't done much acting," she continued, "but I promise I'm going to give this one hundred and ten percent. More even!" And then she did something unprecedented in the history of our battling groups.

She hugged me.

Granted, it wasn't a substantial hug as Belinda is hardly more than a thin layer of skin on top of bone. She and her sister are so skinny I wonder if they even have internal organs. But the boniness of the hug wasn't remotely the most uncomfortable part. *That* was the expressions on the faces of everyone around me as it happened. Some of the people were jealous that she had been cast. Others were just as shocked as I was, since the tension between Hope and her steps was fairly well-known.

Belinda was so excited that she forgot her traditional subservient role, because she flounced off down the hall without a second thought to Holly and Alexis. If only I could have done the same.

Alexis gave me what I suspect passed for a smile as she followed her twin. There was definitely something of the dark and sinister variety behind that smile. But considering how Alexis has never genuinely smiled at me before, I couldn't be sure. Maybe that's how she always looked when she was happy. The idea made me shudder, and I was glad to feel the warmth return to me after she was gone.

Until I realized that Holly Mayflower was not going anywhere. Her face was much easier to read than Alexis's.

Underneath Holly's mane of hair the color of burning embers was a face that showed nothing but cool resolve. Seriously, the girl didn't have a single blemish. But that's not the point.

"Bryan Stark," she said with a nod, giving me the once over.

"Holly Mayflower," I replied, wondering why we were being so formal.

"Congratulations on being named director of *Achromantic*," she said.

"Thank you," I said, trying to match her tone as best I could. "Congratulations on getting the lead in Mr. Randall's play."

"Thank you," she said with forced politeness.

We stood in the middle of the hall in silence while I worried for my safety. I don't know why. I hadn't done anything wrong. Some people might even go so far as to say I actually did something nice.

But Holly was not some people.

"If you," she said, "in any way"—she glared—"did this to make Belinda look like a fool or to sabotage her or to do anything to hurt her *at all*, I will make it my life's purpose to punish you." Go figure. Holly Mayflower actually cared about one of her friends.

I wanted to tell her that she was way off base in her suspicion and that threats were certainly unnecessary, but I was kind of frozen in place. Holly had never directly accosted me before.

It was not a pleasant experience.

The Way of the World

"Bryan," a calm, rational, friendly *adult* voice called out to me. It was Mr. Randall. He was peeking out from his classroom. The fact that he was hiding like a child behind the door didn't quite mesh with the maturity of his voice.

"Yes?" I asked, crossing the hall toward him.

"Didn't I warn you yesterday to stay away from the callboard when the cast list went up?" he asked, waving me into his classroom and shutting the door behind me.

"Um . . . no?"

He actually smacked himself on the forehead like he was in a cartoon—or a V8 commercial. "I'm sorry. I meant to do that. You should give your classmates some time to absorb the cast list before you speak to them."

Sound advice. A little too late, but sound nonetheless.

"It's one of the reason drama classes are scheduled for later in the day," he admitted. I'd always assumed that the schedule was set so that we could continue those classes during lunch or after school. Funny how much of our education has to do with protecting the educators as opposed to teaching the students. Then again, with the turnover rate of some faculty positions, maybe they weren't shielded enough.

"Mind if I hang here until after the bell?" I asked. "To avoid any more halltercations."

"I'll write you a note," he said, reaching for his personalized teacher notepad. One time Gary ripped out half the pages from that pad and wrote up excuse notes to get a bunch of us Drama Geeks out of class for a rehearsal that never was. No one in the school administration ever found out.

Which reminded me . . .

"Thanks," I said as Mr. Randall handed me my excuse note. "Um, Gary asked if he could be my stage manager. I told him that Jimmy is stage managing all three shows, but maybe Gary could be like an assistant stage manager or something?"

Mr. Randall considered the question for a moment, which is something all the better teachers do. The ones with career longevity never answer anything before they've considered it from all angles. "I think it would be a great idea for you to have some extra help since this is your first time directing. Just give me some time to figure out a way to tell Jimmy so that he doesn't think you don't want him as your stage manager."

"Oh, no," I quickly said. "I love working with Jimmy. I just—"

"It's okay," he said. "I understand. But Jimmy can be kind of touchy at times. Especially when he feels like someone is moving in on his territory." Don't I know it? The first time he stage managed the Fall One-Act Festival he made a ninth grader cry just because the poor guy confirmed that it was five minutes to curtain when a senior asked the time.

Thankfully, Hope was the only one who saw me sobbing like a baby.

"Also, Headmaster Collins prefers us to avoid using the term 'assistant' for any roles that the students perform," Mr. Randall said. "He wants everbody to feel like they're on an equal level. Never in a subservient position. So, maybe we can call him the associate stage manager or something."

As long as it meant I got some extra help, we could call him monkey manager and I'd be fine with it.

"How are your friends reacting to the cast list this morning?" Mr. Randall asked, indicating I should get comfortable.

I grabbed the nearest chair and dropped my things on the ground. "Sam's thrilled," I said, leaving out the part where I hadn't actually seen Sam this morning. "Hope? Not so much."

"She'll get past it once she sees Belle in the role," he said.

I couldn't help myself. A burst of laughter popped right out of me. "You don't know Hope."

"But I know you," he said. "You'll make her see it was the best option."

It was nice that my teacher had such confidence in me. Misplaced though it may be. I doubt that anyone had the power to make Hope see clearly on any issues related to her stepsisters. I didn't bother to tell him that.

The halls were clear a few minutes later. I tried to convince

Mr. Randall to let me stay all the way through first period, but he wasn't buying it. A few minutes in to homeroom, he sent me on my merry way. It's amazing how long it takes to get from Mr. Randall's classroom to homeroom. Somewhat less amazing considering I got "lost" several times after making a few turns down wrong hallways.

I was welcomed to homeroom by a few sneers from my classmates and even one thinly veiled "loser" cough. Which I'd never actually heard a girl do before.

I'd like to say things got better once the initial reaction to the call list had passed, but that would be a lie. For the rest of the morning, several of the Drama Geeks in school— particularly from the senior class—shot me looks like they totally blamed me for dashing their dreams by not casting them in Hope's play. More than once I heard mumbling about "casting his best friend" as if Sam weren't one of the two most talented actresses in school and I only gave her a part because I liked her. But not from everyone. I don't want to give the impression that Drama Geeks are nothing but backstabbing haters. Although at Orion Academy we do have more of those than the average high school.

The guys weren't as bad as the girls, because everyone knew Jason was, hands down, the best male actor and I was lucky to have him.

Honestly, it was the third member of my cast that was causing the most buzz. Much of it was shock that this girl, who practically came out of nowhere, got one of the three primo parts in the most sought-after one-act. Belinda wasn't new to the school or anything. We'd been on the same track for years. All the way back to elementary school, in fact. But this acting thing was a recent development. Then again, so was my directing.

Hope was the worst by far. To say things were tense would be quite the understatement. We had most of our classes together, and it was hard to ignore the fact that she pointedly took a chair on the opposite side of the room from me in every one of them. Even the ones where we had assigned seating. Poor Christy Applebaum didn't know what to do when she kept coming into a class and finding her seat had been usurped.

Sam was good, for the most part. She acknowledged that Hope was being unfair since she hadn't even seen Belinda's audition. But Sam was also trying to remain neutral because she is, at heart, a chicken who is just as much afraid of Hope as I am.

But don't tell Sam I called her that, because I'm afraid of *her* too.

The funny thing was that I'd been prepared for all the whispering, the sideways glances, and the conversations with abrupt subject switches as I approached. But I'd expected it about a month and a half earlier. And for a totally different reason.

On the first official day of the school year, I'd woken up to an e-mail that I had been expecting. It even had one of those high priority exclamation marks on it and everything. It was a mass e-mail that had been sent to the entire student mail list. There was no text. Just a picture. Of me kissing a guy on the lips.

Now, my friends and I knew it was just a quick, friendly peck on the lips with Sam's Gay Best Friend, Marq. But the image, frozen in time and sent out with that damn exclamation point, made it seem all the more scandalous.

I'd finally been outed. Not that I'd ever hidden my interest in the masculine sex, but I'd never made the formal announcement that was so en vogue these days. No gathering of my friends to discuss. No formal declaration to my parents. Certainly no cover of *People* magazine with a big ol' exclamation point of its own. I was always one of those people who believed there's no need to ask and there's nothing to tell. Until there was photographic evidence that a whole lot of people would be telling one another about.

So, I got ready for the first day, bracing to be the talk of the school.

It was almost a disappointment to find that I wasn't.

Oh, there were some furtive glances. A couple whispers from the younger kids. I even heard a "Is that him?" But news also broke that morning of yet another accident from a slow-speed paparazzi chase with the celeb du jour. Everyone's attention was kind of split because the celeb was the cousin of one of my classmates. Since most of the student body was preoccupied by the major world event—and seeing how the guy I'd been kissing didn't go to our school and had already left town by the time the photo ran—the "scandal" element had petered out before it even started.

Hope's stepsister Alexis had been the one to send out the photo. I'd expected her to at least keep the story alive, but she'd already moved on to a new tale by first period. In her telling, Alexis's car was nearly sideswiped by the same paparazzi pandemonium, in spite of the fact that said vehicle was parked at school all day for the Back to School Picnic.

It was all so anticlimactic. I'd spent so much time in my life trying to stay out of the spotlight. But the one time I'd been dreading it, I was actually kind of sad to find that I wasn't in it for a bit longer. Everyone in school had been fairly blasé about my same-sex leanings. Nobody even treated me any differently.

But they were treating me differently after the cast list went up.

"Hey, guys," I said as I placed my tray down on our now-regular table in the pavilion where my friends and I lunched. More than a lunchroom, the pavilion was an outdoor covered deck with great views of the Pacific Ocean.

"Hey," Sam and her boyfriend, Eric Whitman, said in too-cute unison. Their arms were intertwined in a manner that must have made eating difficult. At least they weren't sharing a milkshake with two straws like in some hokey fifties movie.

I'd come to terms months ago with Sam and Eric being a couple. They were in it for the long haul . . . or until graduation at the very least. Just because I'd accepted their status as a permanent couple didn't make the cloying PDAs any more tolerable.

I looked down to the quiet one at the other end of the

table, hoping to find a kindred spirit to make fun of the sappy couple with me. But he didn't even raise an eyebrow when I arrived.

"Hello," I said to my best friend turned enemy turned friend turned apparent stranger, Drew Campbell.

"Hi," he mumbled without picking his head up from whatever he was writing.

"Homework?" I asked him.

No response.

This was getting ridiculous. I kind of lied earlier when I said there wasn't much of a reaction at school about my start-of-the-year outing. There was a reaction. One. The friendship that had been rekindling between me and Drew over the summer had taken a decidedly colder turn. At first I'd chalked it up to Eric's return from summer vacation. Eric had replaced me as Drew's best friend years earlier. It was only natural that he'd reclaim his spot when he got back in town. But I didn't expect to get dropped so totally.

Not that Drew was no longer around. As mentioned earlier, Eric and Sam were kind of attached. Since I was semiattached to Sam, and Drew was equally attached to Eric, we spent a lot of time together, but not really together. The level of banter that Drew and I had previously engaged in had not been the same at all. And the more time we spent together, the more awkward things got.

It wasn't much of a leap for me to figure out why the dynamic had changed.

I turned to the lovebirds. "What's up with him?"

"He's freaking about the essay for his college apps," Eric replied.

"Already?" I asked.

They both shrugged. In unison. *How adorable!*

Bleh.

Granted, it was late October and we all should have been in the same position with the early college deadlines looming. But I wasn't really worried. I was applying to UCLA. My grades were good. I was a local resident. And my grandpa had a reading room in one of the libraries named after him. True, it's not an entire building, but with Orion Academy on my transcript, I was pretty much a shoo-in to get in. Seeing how Drew's grandfather has the room next door to Grandpa's, I figured he was in the same shape.

As kids Drew and I had always talked about going to UCLA together. Even though we'd grown apart since then, I knew he wasn't looking to flee the area as soon as he graduates. Like me, he actually likes his family. And also like me, Ivy League would put a slight strain on his parents' financial arena, but we can both easily afford UCLA.

Unlike, say, Eric who not only could afford to go through to a doctorate in Ivy League schools but also had gotten a full scholarship based on his soccer-playing abilities.

Because, you know, life is so fair.

I chose to ignore the person ignoring me and focus on my lunch. Things were unusually quiet at our table, which is when I realized that the other wheel in our group, Hope, was nowhere to be seen. It was kind of a relief. Being with her during lunch, when we had limited teacher supervision—and protection—was something I'd been dreading all morning.

I was even more thankful for her absence when Belinda stepped up to our table with her tray. "Hi, Bryan," she said. A look immediately passed between Sam and me. Belinda wasn't sitting down or anything, but I wondered if she was waiting for an invitation. Not that it would ever come. If Hope walked in to find her stepsister sitting at our table . . . I shudder to think.

"Hi," I said as tentatively as I could say a word that has only two letters.

Then there was a rather dramatic pause while we all considered what to say next. Even Drew peeked up from his essay to see how this one played out.

"So, where is rehearsal this afternoon?" Belinda asked. "Are we in Hall Hall?"

"Um . . ." I hadn't actually talked to Mr. Randall about that yet. We were both too busy cowering in his classroom this morning to have a productive conversation. "Since Jason is out, I thought we should put it off till tomorrow. Don't want to start without my full cast."

"Okay," Belinda replied with a smile suggesting that she agreed with my plan. "I'll go home and start memorizing the script."

"Actually," I said, aware that everyone in the area was watching this interaction. "Don't. I'd like to do a read-through first."

Belinda nodded her head. "Good idea," she said. "Don't

want me getting locked in to anything before we go over it together. Makes sense."

To say that I was surprised she had that much insight into the process would be an understatement. I don't know what came over me, but with her tray still sitting on our table, I was almost inclined to ask her to join us. Thankfully, Holly and Alexis came up, saving me from making the massive faux pas.

"Hey," Holly said. "We're sitting with my cast today. Over there."

"Sure," Belinda said, turning her tray in the other direction. "Bye."

Sam's and my eyes followed as the trio of terror made its way across the pavilion toward the side that overlooked the ocean.

"Huh," Sam said. "Not even a full day and already they're *Holly's* cast."

"Don't even think of it," I said. "You're in *my* cast. You're not getting top billing on this one."

"I'm perfectly fine taking the backseat," she said. "Don't want anyone to go blaming me for certain casting decisions."

"Belinda's really excited about her part," Eric said, picking up on the unspoken topic. "She was talking all about it in sociology. I was kind of surprised you put her in the play."

"She gave the best audition," I automatically replied. It was the first time I said it without feeling defensive.

"I'm sure Hope bought that argument," Drew unexpectedly chimed in.

Before I could respond, Gary joined us at the table. "So?" he asked eagerly.

"Mr. Randall is cool with it, but we've got to wait until he tells Jimmy," I said.

"All right!" he replied with a fist pump in the air.

This caused Sam to raise an eyebrow in my direction.

"Gary's going to be our associate stage manager," I explained.

Drew interrupted. "Associate?"

"Don't ask," I said. "And don't tell Jimmy yet. Mr. Randall wants to make sure he's okay with it before it becomes official. You know how touchy Jimmy gets."

"Not everyone cries when Jimmy yells at them," Sam said.

"You didn't even go here back then!" I said. *Oh wait.* "I don't know what you're talking about!"

Company

I slid the three wooden chairs into a row in the center
of the room and placed the fourth chair facing them. It was a
very schoolmarm way of seating.

I tried them in a circle, but it looked so square.

Then I tried two rows of two facing each other, but it felt
like we were on a train to nowhere.

I was just about to fit them one behind the other in a conga
line when Gary came into the room. "Hey, I was supposed to
do that."

"Sorry," I said, leaving the chairs in a semiscattered position. We were in Sam's mom's classroom. Anne had lent it
to us since Mr. Randall was working with his cast in the
drama room and Ms. Monroe had hers in Hall Hall. The
three of us directors would rotate rooms every day through
the weeks leading up to the show. My teachers had offered
me the auditorium for our first rehearsal, but I figured the

read-through of Hope's play would be better in a more intimate space.

Since English was my last class of the day, I'd stuck around while everyone went back to their lockers, and busied myself by pushing chairs around. Anne kept her desks in a circle around the edge of the room, so we already had a nice empty space in the center. Which gave me plenty of time to play musical chairs without any tunes.

"I needed an outlet for my nervous energy," I explained.

"What's to be nervous about?" Gary asked as he pulled a fifth chair into the grouping and slid them all into a better circular formation than I had managed. "It's just a read-through. All you have to do is sit back and listen. They're actors. You could probably fall asleep and they wouldn't notice until you didn't applaud at the end."

"Says the fellow actor," I reminded him.

"Associate stage manager, if you please," he said with a flourish and a bow. "And now I shall start associating." He took some freshly copied *Achromantic* scripts from his bag and laid them out on the chairs, careful to leave each one at an informal angle.

While he finished up his strategically unstrategic placement of the scripts, Hope came in and handed him a second stack. "Here," she said. "Use these instead."

Gary looked to me and I held up a hand to stop him from taking them. "What are those?"

"New version," she said. "I reworked it last night. This is better."

"Correct me if I'm wrong," I said, "but didn't Mr. Randall talk to you about rewriting your play? And didn't we agree to lock in the final version before we had auditions?" Hope has a tendency to work and rework a piece so much that her writing rarely looks the same from day to day. She was constantly turning in new pages to her creative writing teacher days after an assignment was due. Poor Mr. Swanson had to start grading her on a sliding scale, dropping one point for every new revision she made him read. Since her work tends to start out with a 100, it's not like the change in grade is all that dramatic.

"That was before I saw who was in the cast," Hope said. "I had to make some changes to allow for the weaknesses of some of the actors."

"Some of" being Belinda of course.

Not even one minute into my first rehearsal and already I was facing a challenge to my role as director. As much as I wanted to give my friend the benefit of the doubt that she wasn't intentionally trying to undermine my position, I also had to exert my power or else everyone would start walking all over me. It probably would have been easier if Gary weren't standing between the two of us like our own private audience.

"Or," I said diplomatically, "you can wait to see how things go through the rehearsal process."

"Or," she replied, "you can look over the new script and give me your opinion then."

"Or," I insisted, "you can trust me to be the director you asked me to be."

The pause she took in response was infinitesimal, yet it

somehow managed to stretch on forever until she looked down at her scripts and said, "Fine. But I'm holding on to these, and if the cast can't handle their parts, we're switching to these before opening night."

"Fine," I said, giving in slightly as she took the chair that I'd scoped out for myself. Gary quickly slid another chair into the circle without comment.

"This must be the place," Jason MacMillan said with a scratchy-sounding throat as he entered the room. He came right up to me, thrusting his right hand in my direction. I looked down at it quizzically. "Always shake hands with my director on the first day of rehearsal. Thanks for waiting a day for me to get back."

"No problem," I said, taking his hand, hoping that he wasn't still contagious from whatever he had the day before. This was likely the first of many of Jason's superstitious rituals I'd have to deal with before the show was over. But as long as he gave me the performance we usually got out of him, it was well worth putting up with the eccentricities.

As he moved to shake Hope's hand—starting a new tradition of shaking hands with the playwright—my associate stage manager impressed me even more by passing me a small bottle of antibacterial hand sanitizer. "Smooth," I said as I wiped away any lingering germs.

Germ free and ready to go, I was glad to see Sam coming into her mom's classroom with her determined face on. I wasn't so happy to see that she had brought an entourage. Actually, seeing them behind her in matching shirts with the word "Hollister" plastered across them, they looked more like preppie backup singers.

"You don't mind if Eric and Drew sit in on rehearsal?" she asked as the guys hung by the doorway. Honestly, I kind of did. Not because I still had any issues with them. I didn't need the additional pressure of holding my first rehearsal in front of an audience. Since we were only going to be reading through the play, I figured it wouldn't hurt. But I also didn't want to set any kind of precedent. Soccer practice didn't start until mid-November. I wasn't planning on being their time filler until then.

"Fine with me," I lied, flashing a smile in their direction. Eric returned it in kind. Drew kept his eyes down on the floor.

"We'll stay out of the way," Eric said as he led Drew to a pair of desks in the back corner. Drew didn't seem like he wanted to be around me at all, but he wasn't saying anything. I don't know. Maybe I was making more out of it than was really there. But Drew certainly did seem to be pulling away again. And this time there wasn't any college application essay in front of him to blame for the distraction.

"I'm not late, am I?" Jimmy Wilkey asked as he buzzed into the room. "I mean, I know I'm late, because I'm usually the first to arrive at a rehearsal, but I didn't know I was supposed to be here. I thought you had everything under control." He threw a not-so-subtle, not-so-friendly glance in Gary's direction. "But Mr. Randall suggested I sit in today, just to see if you needed anything. Or to help Gary get acclimated to the *associate* stage manager position."

Oh great. A spy. Jimmy would go back and report every second of the rehearsal to our teacher. And being Jimmy, everything that he said would be heightened beyond actual reality. Just what I needed.

Before I could respond to the latest surprise, Gary suavely stepped in with a big, bright smile. "Thanks, Jimmy," he said, eyeing the collection of chairs in the center of the room. "I was kind of nervous with this being my first day and all. I could use a guy with your experience to keep me on the right track. Make sure you've got my back."

For me, he was laying it on a little thick, but Jimmy was eating it up.

"Oh, okay," Jimmy said. "I'll just hang back out of the way." Jimmy saw Eric and Drew sitting over in the corner and shot me a disapproving look before taking a desk on the opposite side of the room. Gary flashed me a conspiratorial smile. I'm guessing he was particularly glad that Jimmy offered to stay out of the way as we'd run out of single chairs in the room and Gary would have had to search one down unless he was going to be stuck behind a desk.

There was still one empty chair in the collection at the middle of the room. I tried my best not to glance at the clock because I saw that Hope was staring at it intently while letting out annoyed huffs of breath every few seconds.

"Sorry," Belinda said, entering five and a half huffs later. "I thought we were in the auditorium."

"That's okay," I said, daring a glance at the clock. "You still have a minute before we dock your pay."

There was confusion in her eyes.

"That's a joke."

"Oh," she said . . . nervously. It was weird. I don't know if I've seen any member of the trio of terror nervous before. As she glanced over her shoulder, I saw that her sister, Alexis, had come in behind her.

"Hi," I said. "I'm going to keep her for about an hour today." The play was only about thirty-five minutes long, but I was leaving time for discussion. I assumed Alexis wanted to know when to come back to pick up her sister.

Silly me.

"You don't mind if Alexis watches?" Belinda asked. "Hope's our ride home."

"It's a closed rehearsal," Hope said.

Alexis's head swiveled around the room to Eric, Drew, and Jimmy. "Doesn't look closed to me."

"It's okay," I said, for no reason at all since she was already moving toward a desk beside Drew. I felt better when he didn't bother to acknowledge her as she came over.

But I had other things to worry about when I realized that every single head in the room—but Drew's—was turned in my direction, waiting for me to get things started.

"Um . . . hi," I said, standing in the center of the room with almost everyone's eyes on me. A speech seemed like it was in order. Maybe something inspirational. Something to get my cast excited for the challenge ahead of us. Mr. Randall always opened his first rehearsal with a quote about theater from some famous historical figure. But all I could come up with was

"Uneasy lies the head that wears the crown." (*Aside:* Shakespeare's *King Henry IV, Part* 2.) And while it was appropriate for my mood, I doubted anyone would find it the least bit inspirational.

I should have had Hope write something for me, though with her current mood I would have been afraid to see what she would come up with. Something bitingly sarcastic and dripping with subtext, I'm sure.

"Let's get started," I said. It may have lacked emotional resonance, but at least it provided direction. "You've all got your scripts for the read-through. And since the writer has graced us with her presence"—and a glare in my direction—"I thought maybe Hope would do us the honor of reading the stage directions along with the actors performing the dialogue?" My voice went up into another pitch as I ended the question with a more pleading tone than I'd intended.

"Fine," Hope said as everyone flipped to the first page of the original script.

I sat down and opened my own script, prepared for the read-through to begin.

"'*Achromantic,*'" Hope said at the same time Belinda started her opening line.

"Oh," Belinda said, her face going red. "Sorry. I didn't . . ."

"That's okay," I said, placing what I hoped was a reassuring hand on hers. "I think we're all a bit nervous."

"I'm not," Hope said pointedly.

"Well, I am," I said. Not that the actors wanted to hear that their director was a bag of nerves, but Belinda seemed to find it somewhat reassuring. "Let's start again."

I looked to Hope, silently begging her not to screw up my first rehearsal.

"'*Achromantic*,'" she said. "'By Hope Rivera.'"

Sam and I aimed smiles of pride at our friend. We were about to begin the first official rehearsal of the play she wrote. In three weeks, this cast was going to perform it in front of an audience. We were all aware of the momentous moment, and I felt the tension in the room ease ever so slightly.

"Sounds like a bad slasher film," Alexis said just above a whisper.

This time Belinda paled, but the rest of us chose to ignore it.

"'Offstage,'" Hope said at the same time that Belinda once again said her first line.

This evoked a groan from Hope that was loud enough to make even Drew's head pop up. "I'm reading the stage directions," she said harshly to Belinda.

Belinda apologized again. "I didn't know you were going to read that."

"Well, it's a stage direction," Hope said. "Bryan said I was going to read the stage directions."

"Yes," Belinda said, shying away from her stepsister. I could see Alexis's body clenching at her desk. She was ready to pounce. "But I didn't know you read the small stuff like that."

This time I decided not to say anything. I sent a pleading look toward Hope, who took my message and started again.

"'*Achromantic*,'" she said, sounding less and less excited with each reading. "'By Hope Rivera.'" Then she took an excruciatingly long pause, like she was daring Belinda to speak. This time I glared at Hope. "'Offstage,'" she said.

"I just love calla lilies when they're in bloom," Belinda said as if she were calling from offstage. "I only wish I had a vase to put them in. . . ."

Hope let out another huff, like she had some problem with the line read. Maybe I was being defensive for having cast Belinda, but it sounded perfectly fine to me. I guess Hope got over the annoyance, because she continued reading the stage directions. "'The curtain opens on the apartment of a young artist . . .'"

And we're off!

I'd read Hope's play enough times to know already that it was totally brilliant. Now that it had actual actors in the parts, it was freakin' amazing.

Achromantic is the story of the aforementioned young artist, Mackenzie (Jason), who is on the brink of superstardom in the art world. There's a love triangle between him and his live-in girlfriend, Rachel (Belinda), and the "other woman," Felicia (Sam). Felicia is the bookkeeper Mackenzie recently hired to handle his quickly expanding finances . . . and who also happens to be Rachel's sister. (I know! Drama!) It's an allegory for the conflict between the creative and logical sides of the brain with great insight into both minds.

Unlike the writings of many people our age, it isn't some thinly veiled story about Hope's own life at all. It isn't the story of her first kiss with a girl, which happened this past summer. It isn't some bitter rant about the end of her parents' marriage, which wasn't nearly as dramatic as most high-profile L.A. divorces. No. This story was totally new and unique and utterly heart wrenching.

My heart was particularly wrenched hearing it aloud for the first time. I had no doubt that Sam and Jason would work wonders with the material. But Belinda was the real surprise. Her audition hadn't been a fluke. She actually was good. As my cast read, I subtly scanned the room to make sure I wasn't deluding myself into believing in Belinda's talent just because it would make my life easier.

I wasn't.

All of our uninvited guests were following along with the read-through, thoroughly engrossed. Eric was practically leaning over his desk to make sure he didn't miss a word. Jimmy wasn't shaking nearly as much as he usually does. Even Alexis removed the permanent scowl from her face and almost seemed moved by the play. We were all thoroughly entertained.

Well, everyone except . . .

"She's chicken necking," Hope interrupted in the middle of Belinda's big monologue. And, granted, she was right. Belinda's head was leaning forward with each word that she emphasized in her speech. So named because it resembled a chicken picking at some feed.

I held up a calming hand to the novice actress, who was utterly confused by the foreign term. I quickly gave her a summary of what she was doing, adding that "We'll work on it later."

Belinda continued her way through the monologue, her head bobbing slightly as she went.

"She's doing it again," Hope said.

I smiled in a forced way. "Thank you, Hope. We'll work on it later. I want to get through the read-through first."

"Fine," Hope said. "I just thought it would be good to train her out of the bad habits before they stick. But you're the director. I only wrote the damn thing."

"I'm sorry, Hope," Belinda said. "I'll work on it."

And even though I believed her and I knew she was trying, Belinda's head bobbed forward again a couple lines later. This earned her a loud, dramatic sigh from Hope, which nearly prompted Alexis out of her seat to defend her sister.

But, oddly, Sam was the first to react. "Okay, Hope. We get it. Move on." Then she put a hand out and nearly touched Belinda, before she came back to her senses and stopped herself. We tried to avoid physical contact with the evil trio at all possible times. "You're doing good so far," she said. The "so far" was added more for Hope's benefit, but whatever. It got us moving forward again and took us to the end of the play. And everyone continued to be enthralled right on up to Hope's reading the final stage direction.

"'Mackenzie and Felicia freeze midfight. Even though Rachel is only in the other room, their passion can no longer be deterred. Felicia grabs him roughly and pulls him into the kiss that ends any question of how this story will play out. The passion is intense. The heat palpable. But it is more than hot. It is soft. And gentle. And full of deep-rooted love that merges their different personalities into one perfect union. The power of this kiss takes us out of the scene. . . . And curtain.'"

Whoa.

The ending of the play is so intense that it left us all speechless. The three characters explode into a window-shattering fight that culminates in the . . . well, you read about the kiss. It was going to be the hardest part of the show to stage. The challenge I'd been dreading since I first read it. If I blew it, it wouldn't matter what happened in the prior thirty-five minutes. No one would remember anything but the lackluster ending.

I had total faith in my actors to pull it off. Sam and Jason were ready for the challenge. Though maybe there was a hint of embarrassment there as well. They were kind of staring pointedly down at their scripts. And maybe a bit red around the tops of their ears. Not only were they going to have to pull off this amazing kiss as scripted but they were going to have to do it in front of an auditorium full of classmates, faculty, and parents.

And then I realized one more thing as I looked past Sam to see the expression on Eric's face. It was the first time he was hearing how the play ended. And he clearly didn't like it.

State of the Union

"Thanks again," I called out as my cast and their entourages exited the room, leaving me behind with my associate stage manager and playwright. "That went pretty well," I said to them.

Hope responded by handing me the stack of new scripts. "In case you change your mind," she said before making her own exit.

I felt the weight of the scripts in my hands while weighing the options for my next move. It wouldn't hurt to page through them and see what changes Hope had in mind. "What's with that?" Gary asked before I could flip a page.

"Oh, you know . . . Hope and her stepsisters. They kind of hate each other," I said, dropping the scripts by my bag so I could help Gary move the chairs back off to the side.

"Everyone knows that," he said lightly. "Belinda didn't do so bad."

"True," I said. "But Hope is right. We will need to work on that chicken-necking problem with her."

"This is the first real play she's ever been in," he reminded me. "Give her a chance."

"I will," I said, feeling defensive for some reason. "I'm just trying to figure out what I need to focus on as a director. You know, the big stuff. Like that kiss at the end. That's going to take some work to get right." Then I added cryptically, "And some finessing."

"You caught the tension too, then?" Gary asked, deciphering my cryptic comment with lightning speed.

"Wait. He was sitting behind you. How did you—"

"It was like all the air went out of the room," Gary said. "That's going to be a problem. I can feel it."

"Nah," I said, for my benefit more than for Gary's. The last thing I needed were *more* personal problems getting in the way of the production. "Eric knows it's only acting. He'll be fine."

Gary looked like he wasn't as sure about that as I was trying to sound.

"Besides, the kiss doesn't come till the end of the play," I reasoned. "We've got a lot of rehearsing to do before we get to that."

"True," Gary said, putting the last chair in place. We both checked to make sure no one had left anything behind. Didn't want to leave any mess for Anne in the morning since she was doing us a favor by lending the room. "You want to grab some coffee?"

"I've got to go update Mr. Randall on how rehearsal went," I replied.

"Like Jimmy isn't doing that as we speak."

"True," I said right back at him. "All the more reason I should do damage control." It's not that Jimmy would intentionally say anything bad about me. It's just that in his exuberance he sometimes makes things seem more dramatic than they really are. I could already hear him breaking down the whole Hope-and-Belinda episode into a raging fight that I hadn't managed to get under control.

Not that it couldn't become that, but we weren't there yet.

"Then I'll see you tomorrow," he said. "And tomorrow and tomorrow and tomorrow."

"Adieu," I replied as we both gave each other exaggerated bows.

I found myself actually smiling on the way to meet with Mr. Randall. Minor tensions aside, the first read-through went pretty well. Sam and Jason were going to be stellar in their parts and I had no doubt that Belinda could come along as well. With Gary on my team, I knew the technical side of my rehearsals were going to run smoothly. And Hope may have been an irritating grain of sand in the oyster, but she'd already delivered her pearl of a script, so her involvement was kind of done. If we—meaning I—could keep her interference to a minimum, we could have smooth sailing to opening night.

Of course, any number of things could happen along the way, throwing our production into a frenzied state of catastrophe and leaving us with nothing but tears and recriminations. Because recriminations *always* come with tears. I figured the recriminations would be directed *at* me and the tears coming *from* me. But I preferred to look on the bright side. Hope could always kill me before it got to that.

Somehow, the smile I'd had a moment earlier was gone. It didn't come back when I got to Mr. Randall and found that not only had his rehearsal ended but Jimmy was right where I knew he'd be, giving our teacher a full play-by-play of events. I politely listened to him wrap up. Although, some might call what I was doing "eavesdropping" since neither of them knew I was around. Once Jimmy was done I made my presence known. Jimmy didn't even seem embarrassed, but why would he? In his mind he wasn't gossiping, he was simply doing his job.

"Hey, Bryan," Jimmy said. "Thanks for letting me sit in on your rehearsal."

I plastered that smile back on my face and gave him two sarcastic thumbs up. "Thanks for coming!"

He looked confused but didn't say anything. Which was a normal state for Jimmy. Once he left I set the record straight for Mr. Randall, acknowledging that, *yes*, there was some tension, but *no*, my teacher did not need to step in. Considering the Hope/Belinda problems were kind of expected, Mr. Randall only gave a few words of advice before telling me to go home.

The advice? Make it work.

Suddenly, my teacher had become Tim Gunn from *Project Runway*.

After I left the theater I realized that I didn't want to go home where I would be alone till my mom got there. I was too buzzed. I'd survived my first rehearsal with minimal damage to my psyche and my ego. I wanted to celebrate.

I tried to catch up with Gary to see if he still wanted to get coffee, but he was gone. Sam wouldn't be home yet, and she didn't have a cell phone I could call to find her. And I wasn't about to bother Hope. I was still letting her calm down a bit. Out of desperation I almost tried Drew but figured there wasn't any point.

When I struck out with the friends my own age, I tried the one my parents' age. Mom may have been at the Melrose store, but Blaine was covering the afternoon shift at Li'l Beaches only a few minutes away. I hopped in Electra and made my way to the store, which I found unusually empty.

"Hello?" I called out, expecting an echo. It was odd that there were no customers in the store, especially one day after a new shipment came in. But it was downright bizarre that there was no staff. "Helloooooo?"

"Hey," a voice said from behind me, causing me to jump like an overcaffeinated Chihuahua. Turning, I found the six feet whatever and two hundred and fifty pounds of muscle that was Blaine standing in the doorway with what was probably a chai tea latte in his hand.

"You left the store unattended?" I asked. "You'd probably kill me if I left the store unattended."

"One: I can see the store from the coffee shop on the

corner there," he said. "And two: I would *definitely* kill you if you left the store unattended."

"Hypocrite," I said.

"I'm bigger than you," he reminded me. "I can afford to be a hypocrite. And thanks for coming by. There must be a two-for-one spa day in the area or something because we've had no customers in here all day and I am bored out of my skull."

"Good," I said. "Because I was hoping for a captive audience."

While Blaine sipped his tea, I regaled him with tales of my first official day as director. As per my usual storytelling endeavors, I embellished freely, skipping over the negative parts because I didn't need to talk to Blaine about all that. Yet.

He listened attentively, didn't comment when he sensed that I was skipping parts (because he's scarily psychic with me), and clapped me on the back when I was done. From Blaine that was the highest form of praise. "Congratulations," he said. "I hope you being a big-time director now doesn't mean you're above helping out at the store."

"I am still second assistant manager," I said with pride. "You've got me until my first film deal."

"Good to know," he replied. "Because I need to get all the new stock organized in the back room. Can you watch the front for the rest of the afternoon?"

Drat. I'd let my guard down. Usually I could tell when he was walking me into a trap. "Sure," I said reluctantly. Since there was no one around to celebrate my success with, I might as well help out. Besides, I could use the extra cash. I clocked in, wished Blaine luck as he disappeared into the back, and proceeded to be bored as hell.

Blaine wasn't kidding when he said the store wasn't getting a lot of foot traffic. After a half hour alone stocking the shelves with the new puppy-ween costumes, I found myself getting slaphappy. That's the only way to explain why I thought it would be fun to try on an extralarge jack-o'-lantern dog hat.

Figures that's what I'd be doing when Drew unexpectedly walked in.

I don't know who was more uncomfortable in that moment. Okay. I do. And it wasn't the one with a puffy pumpkin on his head.

I slipped the costume off my head and replaced it with my fedora, then went over to greet our customer. "Hey."

Yes, I am a man of few words.

Drew nodded, which proves that he's a man of even fewer.

"Do you need something?" I asked.

"I didn't think you'd be working this afternoon," he replied.

I could take a few minutes to dissect that statement, but it pretty much spoke for itself. He only came because he was under the impression that I wasn't going to be here. But why?

"Can I help you?" I asked, waiting for something. *Anything*.

He sighed like my help was the last thing he wanted. "My parents are getting Casey a dog for her birthday."

"Really?" I asked. Drew's sister has wanted a dog ever since she could say the word "dog." I wondered why now. I wanted to ask "why now?" But I didn't. There used to be a time when

I wouldn't have to ask those kinds of things. Drew would kindly fill in the blanks on his own. This? Not one of those times.

"We don't sell dogs here," I said, hoping to get a rise out of him. We hadn't been best friends for years, but even when we weren't speaking all that much, we were always good with the banter.

"I know," he said.

That's all he said.

He was really making me work for this. "And . . . do you want to get something *for* the dog?" I asked.

He gave me a nod with a sort of half shrug that I took to mean yes. Seriously. We were both seniors. Weren't we supposed to be out of the sullen phase by now? Isn't there some kind of time limit on these things?

I could have asked what kind of dog they were getting or what type of gift he had in mind, but I didn't. I just walked him over to a display of our most popular chew toys, handed him the top sellers, and rang him up. He left with a mumbled "bye."

"What's with him?" Blaine asked, coming out from the back room.

"It's not nice to eavesdrop," I said.

"Now who's being the hypocrite?" he asked, being the person who knows me better than anyone. "So, what *is* going on with him?"

"Beats me," I said. "He's been like that ever since . . ." I couldn't say it out loud.

"Ever since you came out?" Blaine finished my thought, as he so often does.

Let me quickly bring you up to speed on that. . . .

Shortly after my particular leanings became, ever-so-briefly, the talk of the school, I figured it was important to let my parents know before they heard it through the Malibu grapevine. The best way, I felt, to do that was by leaving a Web page up on my computer that was all about "How to Tell Your Parents." I made sure Blaine saw it, knowing that he'd tell my mom. She and Dad arranged for a call since he was away in Timbuktu or some such place that his mysterious job took him to. That way I didn't have to bring it up myself and none of us was surprised by the news. I guess you could say that I sort of came out to my parents by proxy. It was also done on a conference call. Like I said, this is Malibu.

"Give Drew time," Blaine said. "He's had an image of who you are pretty much since you were born. You're still that person, but some people have trouble seeing that."

The problem was that Drew has had time. He's had more time than anyone else.

And his attitude hasn't changed one bit.

Waiting in the Wings

Hall Hall.

The school auditorium seemed much larger than ever before. Much, much larger than it actually was. It's funny. I'd been on the stage many times over the years as an actor. I'd been on it in shows. I'd been on it for auditions. I was on it on what was probably the second worst day of my life when famed producer-director-actor-writer-songwriter-choreographer Hartley Blackstone decided that I was such a bad actor I didn't even rate a critique. But standing there by myself in an empty auditorium before my first official blocking rehearsal . . . I suddenly felt very, very small. Insignificant even.

"Hey, boss!" Gary called as he came down the aisle. When he reached the stage, he gave a deep bow all the way to the floor, as if he were kneeling before royalty.

"Get up before somebody sees you," I said, even though the ego stroke couldn't have come at a better time.

"That's how I know you're going to be a good director," he said. "No power tripping."

I let out an exaggerated sigh. "How are you going to get me coffee if you're bowing and scraping on the ground? Though you could polish my shoes while you're down there."

"Your wish is my command," he said as he joined me onstage. If only more people acted that way around me.

"You ready?" Gary asked.

"As I'll ever be," I replied.

And then began the parade down the center aisle.

First came Jason, blessedly alone.

Sam was not far behind, along with Eric and Drew. The former was attached at her arm. The latter had his eyes so focused on his feet that I was surprised he didn't veer into the seats.

Then came Hope.

Followed by Belinda.

Followed by Alexis.

Followed by Holly.

HOLLY?

"Holly," I called out as she made her way down the aisle. "You're rehearsing in the drama room today."

"No, I'm not," she said as she continued her way into a row and sat beside Alexis. "Mr. Randall's only working the first few pages today. I don't come in until later. Since I don't have any-where better to be, I figured I'd sit in on Belle's rehearsal. That is, if you don't mind."

If I did mind, I'd have to mind Eric and Drew also.

Somehow, I didn't think that one would go over so well. "Fine," I said. At least Jimmy hadn't shown up.

At which point the auditorium door opened once more.

But it wasn't Jimmy. It was Suze Finberg.

"Sorry I'm late," she yelled as she scurried down the aisle. Considering I hadn't been expecting her, I can't really say that she was running behind.

I looked to my associate stage manager to see if he knew what was going on.

"My bad," he said. "Suze's costume designer for the shows. She wanted to swing by before the production meeting to check things out."

I merely nodded. It was already more of an audience for my first true rehearsal than I'd anticipated. One more person didn't make much of a difference. The announcement that Suze was doing costumes was met with general enthusiasm from the group. Holly and Alexis in particular seemed to be excited by the news. So excited that Holly was soon pushing Alexis out of her seat and directing her up the aisle. Alexis didn't seem too interested in her commander's directions, but she did as she was told and left the auditorium for parts unknown.

This worried me for reasons I could not identify.

I filed the unusual behavior in the back of my mind so I could start our rehearsal. Once again I felt an urge to speechify. And once again nothing came to mind. "Okay," I said. "Could my cast please separate from their entourages and join me onstage?" When stressed I go for sarcasm.

Jason, Sam, and Belinda left the audience and made their way up to me. For some reason Hope took the invitation to include her as well. I figured it was easier to let her come along instead of risking a scene by telling her to stay where she was. I had a sneaking suspicion that we were going to be in for our fair share of scenes that afternoon. And I wasn't talking about the ones found on the page.

"Okay," I said. "As you know, the action takes place in Mackenzie and Rachel's living room. Gary and I have laid out some chairs to indicate furniture. But we're going to head out to set storage after the production meeting to see what we can find."

"What's this production meeting everyone is talking about?" Belinda asked. "Do I need to be there? Because I didn't know about it." This, naturally, earned a *hmph*-type sound from Hope. I ignored it because Belinda was asking an honest question. If it had come from her sister or Holly, there would have been attitude behind it, like "why wasn't I told?" But there was only curiosity in her tone. And maybe a little embarrassment for not knowing something.

"No," I said. "It's for the directors and tech crew. That's why we're having a shortened rehearsal today. We would have had the production meeting earlier, but Mr. Randall had to schedule things around Ms. Monroe's prenatal doctor visit."

"Ms. Monroe's pregnant?" Belinda asked.

Whoops.

Come to think of it, I wasn't sure if that piece of information was supposed to be kept a secret. No formal announcement had been made about the impending birth. Ms. Monroe only mentioned it the day of auditions because it was part of our conversation about the schedule. She was hardly even showing or anything. Maybe she hadn't wanted the news spread. But she never told me *not* to say anything.

It was too late to take it back. Belinda was already off and running. "Alexis said she was looking heavy—well, Alexis said bloated—but I . . . well, she says everyone looks bloated." That's understandable. Compared to the emaciated Alexis and Belinda, half the starlets in Hollywood are in their nineteenth month of gestation. "A baby! That's great! I guess we know what she was doing on her honeymoon. Did you know she was pregnant, Hope?"

As expected, Hope didn't bother to engage in conversation that was instigated by her stepsister.

But Sam did.

She started by smacking me. "You never told me Ms. Monroe was pregnant."

"Well, I—"

"Hey, guys!" Belinda called out to the gathered audience. "Guess what!"

That was the point I lost control. It was only a couple minutes of gossiping, but we were already working a shortened rehearsal. The chatter carried on a bit longer than it should have when Alexis returned from her mysterious mission and had to be updated on the news. I was more concerned by the satisfied expression on Alexis's face. It rarely bodes well when Holly and friends are happy.

Thankfully, Sam wrapped up all the extraneous conversations with a piercing whistle, and we got back to business.

"Now that we got that out of the way," I said, trying for levity but sounding rather pissy. "Belinda, you're starting off-stage." I pointed stage right, but grabbed on to her when she started to move. I wasn't ready for her to go yet. "Your first line comes before the curtain opens. So I'm going to need you to stand off to the side but in front of the curtain for the line, so you can project—"

"We can't hear you!" Alexis yelled out. I suppose it was my fault she felt she could call out, as I had been pointing in her direction when talking to Belinda about projecting for the audience. Now as I glared at her sister I saw Holly sitting beside Alexis, smiling. If something like that had happened in Mr. Randall's rehearsal, Holly would have immediately demanded that Alexis leave. For me? No such luck. Not that that was a surprise.

"Ignore her," Belinda said as she shot her own glare in her sister's direction. That was a first, as far as I knew. Belinda didn't tend to challenge Alexis like that. Or in any way, really.

I did as Belinda suggested. "We're not going to open and close the curtain today since we don't have time. Just take position and wait for me to tell you to begin."

"Okay," she said with enthusiasm as she made her way off-stage.

"Sam. Jason," I said at a volume slightly louder than normal. I didn't want to encourage any more outbursts from the audience. "I want you two to play around with the opening a bit and try some things out. You're both fighting the feelings you have for each other. You can't keep your hands to yourselves even though your girlfriend, and your sister, is in the next room. We need to feel the attraction from the moment the curtain opens or else the audience is just going to think you're a scummy guy and you're a slut. Hope's script does a great job keeping this from being a soap opera. Now we need to do the same."

"No pressure," Sam said.

I worried I was being too forceful, until Sam cracked a smile. I let out a breath and continued. "We'll be in the audience." I left the stage with Gary and Hope behind me, and we all took seats in the front row. While we were sitting, Jason and Sam took their positions on the two chairs that were doubling as the couch. They were sitting very close together.

"Right now the curtain is closed," I reminded everyone onstage and off . . . and in the audience. "First we'll hear Belinda's line. Then the curtain opens. So the first thing we see is Sam and Jason . . . which is what we're seeing now since the curtain is already open." Yeah, that was some good logic. I studied what was going to be the opening image of the play. Sam and Jason were a little too cozy on the "couch." "I don't know if I want you that close, physically, at the start. We should just suggest it. You kind of look like you're on top of each other."

Sam and Jason overreacted to the inch of space between them, like exaggerated silent movie stars, mugging for the camera as they slid apart.

"I don't think we look on top of each other," Sam said lightly.

"Yeah," Jason agreed. "This is what that would look like." And then he jumped into her lap and pretended to make out with her. The move got a laugh from Alexis and Holly but a lot of silence from the area behind me where Eric was seated.

"Ha. Ha," I said. "Jason, why don't you try standing up and pacing behind her," I suggested, hoping to put some distance between them before Eric snapped.

Jason hopped out of her lap and did what I told him. The new positioning worked for me, so I told them to begin.

Belinda opened the scene from the "kitchen" trying to carry on a conversation while her character's boyfriend and sister performed their mating dance in the living room. Jason and Sam did an excellent job of secret glances and near touches while they struggled to carry on their side of the yelled conversation. I watched, enthralled, as Jason came around to the couch and leaned in for a quick kiss. Their lips barely touched as Belinda stepped into the scene, forcing them to break apart quickly.

"Hold it!" I said.

"Did I do something wrong?" Belinda asked with one foot onstage and one still in the wings.

"What?" I asked. My focus so wasn't on her at the moment. "No. You're fine. I just . . . you're good. I'm concerned about that kiss. We don't need a near miss there. Jason, you and Sam were doing fine up to that part. I liked the little moments you found."

"I don't know," Jason said. "I feel like we're pulling to

each other through the whole open. Like even though it's crazy, I just can't hold back anymore. Maybe we should keep the kiss, but do it earlier and stop it on our own. Before Belinda comes in."

I considered what he was saying. Whenever anyone made a suggestion during Mr. Randall's rehearsals he always took a moment to think it over, even if it was something ridiculous. Jason's suggestion wasn't ridiculous, but I wasn't crazy about it. I figured I should treat my actors with the same respect though. Once enough time had passed, I said, "I want to save the kiss for later. Besides, here it seems a bit . . . cartoonish."

"Very cartoonish," a deep voice behind me echoed. I didn't have to turn to know it was Eric.

"I don't know," Holly, ever the instigator, said. "I think it could be sweet."

"Actually," Hope said. "I wrote it so that we don't see them kiss until the end. It makes that kiss much more powerful."

Suddenly we were directing by committee. I didn't recall asking for additional opinions, yet there they were. Considering Hope's statement of writerly intent put the kibosh on the conversation, I decided to leave it at that.

"Thank you," I said, with a forced smile to my friends and codirectors before turning back to the stage. "Let's run through it again, but without the kiss."

We started over from Belinda's opening line. Sam and Jason re-created their flirtatious dance exactly as they had the first time round, minus the kiss. It worked much better, but I had to stop them again. This time it was to address Belinda, who had been struggling to squeeze herself out from the curtain that was gathered stage right. "When you come into the scene you're going to be carrying tall flowers in an iced tea pitcher," I said. "It's going to be difficult for you to enter from that small space in front of the curtain."

"But you told me to stand here so the audience can hear me when the curtain is closed," she reminded me.

So I did.

"Yes," I confirmed. "When the curtain is closed, I need you offstage but in front of it so the audience can hear you. But while the curtain is opening, is there some way you can quickly run around the back of the curtain so that you'll be behind it when it's all the way open?" She had the oddest blank expression on her face. For a moment I thought I was looking at her twin, Alexis, because she often comes across as clueless. "Am I making any sense?"

"Not really," Holly said.

Thank you, peanut gallery.

"Here, let me show you," I said, getting up from my seat.

Several conversations broke out onstage and in the audience while I got up onstage and walked Belinda through what I was talking about. All I wanted her to do was run around the side of the curtain, so she caught on fairly quick. The only problem was that she was going to have to sneak around the curtain while it was opening from the center and coming toward her. That meant a lot of heavy material would be coming her way on show night. And she really was a tiny wisp of a thing that could easily be taken out by the curtain. We were going to have to rehearse it a few times with the curtain opening to make sure it didn't knock her down. Last thing I needed was an unconscious actress on my hands. Especially on show night. Oh, and it wouldn't be good if Belinda got hurt either.

I gave that note to Gary as I returned to my seat.

"Got it!" He scribbled something into his notepad, positively beaming over receiving his first official director's note. I couldn't help being pulled into his enthusiasm. Here I was, a big-time director, giving notes and everything. Solving the small problem of Belinda's entrance felt like a bigger accomplishment than it honestly was, but it *was* something. The decisions I made were playing out onstage.

I was directing!

Wait. The *best* part was that as soon as I sat back in my seat, all the side conversations ended and everyone gave me their full attention. Without me even asking.

I could like this.

The Cradle Will Rock

The rest of rehearsal went mostly fine. We even managed to get almost to the tenth page of the script . . . if we're defining "almost" as one-quarter of the way through page eight. Hey, it was a shortened rehearsal. I gave my notes to the cast and told them all we'd be back in Anne's classroom for our Friday rehearsal. Gary, Hope, Suze, and I then headed through the backstage exit to the drama classroom where we found Mr. Randall waiting to welcome us at the door.

Make that welcome *three* of us at the door.

"And where do you think you're going?" Mr. Randall asked Hope.

"To the production meeting," she replied.

"Sorry, Hope," Mr. Randall said. "There aren't any other writers coming to the meeting."

"The guys that wrote the plays you and Ms. Monroe are directing are both dead," she reminded him. Not that they would have been coming to a high school production meeting if they'd been alive.

"Be that as it may," Mr. Randall said gently and with total awareness of how powerful Hope's father is, "your job was complete when you turned in the final script. Thank you for your interest, but we'll be fine continuing here without you." It was the nicest way I'd ever heard anyone say "get lost."

Hope paused. Clearly she was debating which battles to choose. If she gave up on this one, it meant I was going to be the one paying for it when it came time to fight with me somewhere down the line. Suddenly, I *really* wanted her to attend this meeting.

"If I leave now, I can catch a ride with Alexis and Belinda," she said. Considering how much she loathed riding home with the steps, I knew I was definitely going to pay for it somewhere down the line.

As Hope hurried off, the rest of us went into the room where Ms. Monroe was already waiting. She was stretched out as much as she could be in a wooden chair that did not recline. She was barely showing, but I could tell she was already in the uncomfortable stage of her pregnancy.

While the rest of the production team settled in, I hurried over to Ms. Monroe for some damage control. "Um . . . Ms. Monroe?"

"Yes, Bryan."

"I kind of accidentally let the cat out of the bag?"

Her brow furrowed. "What cat? And what bag?"

"The one where I sort of may have told everyone . . . well,

everyone at my rehearsal . . . which is actually quite a few people . . . people who like to gossip—"

"Bryan," she said, cutting me off.

"I may have leaked the news that you're pregnant."

"Is that all," she said with a laugh. "You had me worried there was a real problem. That's not a secret. I just haven't made an announcement to the students yet. Alexis was at your rehearsal, wasn't she?" I nodded. "Good. The word will spread on its own."

"You're not mad about not getting to tell them yourself?"

She shrugged. "To be honest, I'm sick of telling people. I come from a very large family."

I took a deep breath of relief as Suze—who'd overheard the conversation—came over to congratulate Ms. Monroe and pepper her with questions.

"How far along are you?"

"Four months."

"Wait. So you—"

"Yes. It's a honeymoon baby."

"That means you're due—"

"In March."

"So you won't be around for spring semester?"

It went on like that for a few minutes, with Gary joining the conversation. Being guys we pretty much let Suze ask all the questions while we nodded at the appropriate intervals.

"Sorry I'm late," Jimmy said, gasping for breath, bolting into the room. I'd been wondering why the meeting was starting off so mellow. "I was stuck in set storage."

"Stuck?" Mr. Randall asked the question on all our minds. With Jimmy that word could mean many different things.

"I was climbing on a dresser trying to get that baby cradle for your play. It was on top of the dresser on a stack of chairs when the whole thing came down on top of me . . . well, around me, really. It was actually kind of cool how it all fell and nothing touched me. Then I was trapped in the middle of a bunch of chairs and couldn't figure out how to get out."

Had anyone else shared this same story, our reaction would have been shock and concern. My teachers would already be filling out incident reports hoping to avoid a lawsuit. But seeing how it was Jimmy—who this kind of thing happened to all the time—the only thing Mr. Randall said was "But where's the cradle?"

Jimmy froze.

I froze too. I knew if I looked at either Gary or Suze we'd all burst out laughing.

"It's okay," I said, focusing on the wall. "I have to go through the storage room after the meeting. I'll grab the cradle while I'm in there."

"Thanks, Bryan," Jimmy said. "I left it on the right side . . . well, more toward the right side of the middle, and kind of in back. Maybe I should draw you a map."

"Or I could just keep an eye out for the pile of chairs," I suggested.

"Or that," Jimmy said.

"Then let's get the production meeting started," Mr. Randall said, taking a seat in the front of the room. "There are a lot of things to go over."

Boy, was that ever an understatement. Nobody ever talks about the unglamorous side of directing. I got to experience that firsthand when the meeting veered off into a five-minute discussion on the proper procedure for exchanging the personal microphones between casts during intermissions. It had been a big deal the previous year when the casts just handed over microphones to their friends and Jimmy had to do a mad search to make sure there were enough to go around for the final play.

And that was only the opening discussion of the meeting. So much went on behind the scenes of the Fall One-Act Festival that I'd never realized before. I couldn't imagine how busy things got during the Spring Theatrical Production, which was a two-night affair of the same two-act play with two different casts . . . with music even.

During this first production meeting we went over preliminary costume ideas with Suze and a list of set pieces and props for Jimmy. We also talked about lighting design because Jimmy's dad was going to supply a freelancer from his production company to help. All that stuff was expected. But then we went on to discuss publicity, ushers, and a whole bunch of other things that I was only partially concerned about . . . or not at all, really. I doubt I needed to be there for half of it, but my teachers were trying to include me as an equal, which was flattering . . . even though I would much rather have gone out to get some coffee.

At the point where my eyes were slowly drooping, I felt Mr. Randall's tone shift. A storm front was coming through the room, which put me on alert. I'd been at Orion Academy long enough to know when a teacher was about to announce something I would not like.

"That brings us to hair," he said.

I wasn't sure what had brought us to "hair," because I'd sort of zoned, but that didn't matter. I couldn't imagine why hair was a meeting topic. I assumed he meant hair*styles*, but I never would have guessed where that topic was going.

"I've had an offer from one of the students," he continued, "to help design the hair for the three plays."

My head dropped down as if all the muscles had gone right out of my neck. I was no longer wondering where Alexis briefly disappeared to during my rehearsal. "Please don't," I said. "I can't . . . please don't."

"Please don't what?" Gary asked.

"Please don't say it," I pled to my teacher. "You already made me cast—"

"*Bryan*," Ms. Monroe warned before I admitted that I was forced to cast Belinda against my will.

"Hope is going to kill me," I said.

"Alexis just wants to help." Mr. Randall confirmed what I already knew he was going to say. "Since the rest of her family is involved."

"Well, please give her my thanks," I said, "but my cast's current hairstyles are perfectly fine for their characters."

"Bryan, all of your actors are playing characters at least a decade older than themselves," Ms. Monroe pointed out. "Don't you think that we can do something with their hair that will help suggest a more mature age?"

"You do realize that Alexis isn't really going to do anything other than hire her personal stylist to come in," I said.

"This is a no-budget production," Mr. Randall replied. "We can use all the professional help we can get."

That statement was true in *so* many ways, but I didn't see how this new member of the production staff was going to make my life any easier.

"If no one has anything else to add . . . ?" Mr. Randall asked.

I felt a subtle jab to my rib cage and turned to Gary.

"The painting," he whispered.

"Painting?" I asked quietly. "Oh, the painting!" I said somewhat louder. Gary was referring to the "piece of artwork that had critics raving about the 'bold new artist' and signified Mackenzie's 'arrival onto the art scene.'" As Hope wrote in the play, it was the one piece that Jason's character refused to sell, no matter how rich it would make him. It was an important image because the script suggested that the art should make a statement about the relationships among the three characters. Hope didn't indicate *how* it commented on the relationships. Guess she was leaving that up to the director. This particular director doesn't know a lot about art, but I was well aware that the piece I was imagining was going to take a real talent.

"Oh, yes," Ms. Monroe said. "I spoke with Mr. Telasco—"

"I should hope," I said. After all, he was the baby daddy.

"—and he's chosen a student to work on the painting," she continued. In addition to being the proud papa, Mr. Telasco was also our art teacher. "It's Drew Campbell."

All the air was sucked out of the room. By me. I saw where this one was going too.

"Drew?" I asked.

First Suze, then *Alexis*, and now . . . Drew? Hail, hail, the gang's all . . . going to drive me insane.

Don't get me wrong, Drew's a great artist. It's just that he hasn't been a *practicing* artist for a few years. I wasn't sure that I wanted my play to be the launching pad for his return to the arts. It would be so much easier to work with someone with a few more years of formal training under his or her belt.

It would be so much easier to work with someone who was speaking to me!

"Wait. Now you want me to make Hope's *ex-boyfriend* part of the production?" I asked, grasping for the one straw that might break this particular camel's back. Yes. I mixed a metaphor there. Sue me.

"Like that's going to be a problem," the traitorous Suze interrupted. "They get along better now than they ever did when they were together."

That was true, actually. They were better friends than lovers. And I still didn't know *why* they'd broken up. But that was a discussion for another time.

"I have a headache," I said, knowing the battle was lost. I wondered what was next. I fully expected to be told that Eric was going to be in charge of selling refreshments during the intermissions. I could not wait for soccer season to start again. On the bright side, my associate stage manager was right there for me with an offer of aspirin. I declined. I was growing fond of the pain.

"Can you make some time to meet with Drew about the painting?" Mr. Randall asked in a way that was more a command than a question.

"I'm on it," I said, all fake smiles.

"Then all that's left is to remind you that we have to cancel rehearsals next Wednesday."

"For Halloween?" Gary asked.

"For Stargazing Night," Mr. Randall said.

"Ohh," all four of us students moaned. It was so unfair that this year Halloween fell on the same night as this incredibly rare, incredibly boring alignment of the planets that Headmaster Collins had deemed perfect for another Stargazing Night.

Don't get me wrong. Having a fully functioning observatory on campus is cool. (*Aside:* Except for when you're intentionally locked inside it. Long story.) Being able to learn about astronomy firsthand looks great on college apps. But Stargazing Night isn't about learning astronomy. It's about "giving back to the community." And that catchy phrase doesn't mean we're doing charity work. It means we're opening up the campus to the wealthy locals in an attempt to ease the pain of having a couple hundred teens and families driving through their neighborhood every day on their way to and from school.

The students try to make a party atmosphere out of the event, but if things start getting too "rambunctious," the headmaster puts a stop to the fun, lest we give our fine neighbors the correct impression of our school. Seeing how attendance was mandatory, not only were we expected to miss out on Halloween festivities this year but we were also going to have to cancel one of our rehearsals so the faculty could prepare.

But since we couldn't do anything to change that, Mr. Randall merely made a note of it and adjourned our very first production meeting; a meeting where the production staff grew by two people who brought a few dozen new issues for me to deal with. I'd always thought the point of production meetings was to make the productions run more smoothly. Somehow, that's not how things worked out for me this time.

Gary grabbed the keys to the set storage room from Jimmy. Okay, well, "grabbed" doesn't quite describe the process it took to get the official stage manager to release them to the *associate* stage manager. It was more like asked, cajoled, begged, threatened, and waited for Mr. Randall to force Jimmy to hand over the keys. But Jimmy finally did. And we were on the way to finding us some set pieces.

I went over my wish list as we walked to set storage. It was quite a bit longer than I'd remembered it. "I hope we can get all this stuff. I don't want to spend my weekend driving to secondhand shops all over town. Our set and prop budget is dismal." You'd think with the amount of money it costs to go to Orion Academy there'd be a bit more money to throw around for school functions. You'd think that, but you'd be wrong.

"Actually," Gary said. "My uncle owns a furniture store."

"A furniture store?" I asked, already knowing this piece of information and hoping that Gary bringing it up meant what I wanted it to mean.

"Okay, a chain of furniture stores," he admitted. "He said we can borrow anything we need."

"Dude, you are a most excellent associate stage manager," I said.

"Dude?" he asked.

"Sorry," I said. "Been hanging out with Eric and Drew a lot lately. More than I want to, really."

"What is the deal with you and Drew anyway?" he asked as we reached set storage.

"Deal?"

Gary worked his way through the many keys on Jimmy's key ring. Leave it to our obsessive, aggressive stage manager to hand over his beloved keys but not tell us which one would unlock the door.

"I thought you guys were like . . . friends again," he said. "But you don't seem to want him involved."

How could I explain the odd relationship between me and my former best friend? Some of it I myself couldn't understand. Some of it I wasn't ready to share with anyone.

"No," I said. "Not friends. It's more like we peaceably coexist."

"Aha!" he said as we both heard the click of the lock. "So it's not like you guys hang out or anything?"

"We did this summer," I said as Gary began the search for

the light switch. I held the door open to give him some light from the hall. "Haven't hung out much since Eric got back from vacation. Why?"

"Just wondering. So, you going to Stargazing Night next week?" he said with a bang and an "Ouch!"

"You okay?"

"Me? Yes. My shin? Not so much. But I'm pretty sure I found the cradle Jimmy came in to get earlier."

"We should have brought a flashlight," I said.

"Yeah," he said. "So, Stargazing Night?"

"I guess," I replied. "It's kind of mandatory, isn't it?"

"That's the impression I got," he said as the light came on, revealing the furniture graveyard better known as the Orion Academy Theater Department Set Storage Area . . . or simply "set storage." It was way more crowded than the last time I'd been in there at the start of summer. Apparently some wealthy alumna (which is kind of redundant) passed away in August and donated the sum contents of her home to the theater department. To fit a mansion into an average school class-room was not a good idea. But it was a good reason not to call the room a "furniture graveyard" anymore.

"Where are you?" I asked, seeing a lot of dark wood but very little of my associate stage manager.

"Over here!" His hand shot out from behind a mirror the size of a barn door.

I made my way through the maze of furniture to him. "Don't think we're going to need to use your uncle's store with all this stuff here," I said.

"I don't know," he replied. "From my vantage point, it looks like we have a choice between ugly seventies or ugly eighties."

"True," I agreed as I banged my head on an avocado green chandelier with big white glass orbs.

"Maybe we should go to the store after school next Wednesday since we don't have rehearsal," he said when I found him standing on top of a molded plastic chair in the shape of a hand.

"Okay," I said. "If we need to." There truly was a lot of crap to choose from in the room. Not all of it was bad. Okay, a lot of it was atrocious, but among the horrors there were actually some nice pieces. My eyes had already fallen on this great armchair that was all worn leather and mangled wood. It was the perfect style for how I imagined the apartment in Hope's script.

"Then we could go to Stargazing Night afterward," he said. "If you want."

"Sounds good," I said as I pointed Gary toward a freaky weird sofa in the shape of a pair of lips. I guess it could be called an object d'art. But I worried about the deceased alumna's taste in body-part furniture.

"If we find any furniture that resembles more-intimate body parts, I'm out of here," Gary said.

"I'm with you there," I agreed as we got down to work.

The Effects of Gamma Rays on Man-in-the-Moon Marigolds

Maybe it was the odd alignment of the planets, but all kinds of weirdness was happening on Halloween. And not the freaky-costumed variety. But that was mainly because we weren't allowed to wear costumes to school. Or to Stargazing Night. But we still managed to get a little loopy in our street clothes.

First of all, my behavior was way out of character. I tend to follow the rules. Obsessively. I do have something of a rebellious side, but that usually exhibits itself in more mundane ways: a snide comment, a whispered questioning of authority. Rarely do I ever outright ignore a teacher's directions. But I did just that when I called an extra rehearsal for Wednesday afternoon even though we'd all been instructed to vacate the building so the faculty could set up for Stargazing Night. Seeing how the observatory was not attached to the main building, and all the festivities were going to be contained to the pavilion and surrounding grounds, I figured no one would mind if me and my cast gathered in Hall Hall for another abbreviated rehearsal.

We'd managed to run through most of the play on Friday, Monday, and Tuesday. The purpose of these first rehearsals was so the cast could move through the space as they developed their characters. Ask questions. Try new things. And then make it all stick by noting the formal blocking in the prompt book. By Tuesday we'd gotten through all but the last two pages. Since I wanted to start working the smaller moments on Thursday, I figured calling a half hour rehearsal to wrap up the blocking wouldn't be the end of the world. Gary and I had unexpectedly found everything we'd needed on our set storage run, so we didn't have to visit his uncle's store. Once those plans were canceled, it wasn't like I had anything else to do.

Which brings us to the second oddity of the afternoon. Things were running incredibly smoothly. Which was crazy since we had the usual assortment of uninvited guests joining us once again. Even Holly was back since Mr. Randall had followed his rules and canceled their rehearsal. But I didn't even mind her being there because she came in with everybody else and sat quietly as we ran through our abbreviated rehearsal. I wasn't sure if it was due to the planetary alignment or dumb luck, but the usual tension that had been present during the first part of the week was now blissfully absent. We were rolling along quite well. I had an answer for every question the cast posed. And they had a response for everything I hit them with. Not only were we ahead of schedule but it also was looking like we were about to wrap up our first uninterrupted rehearsal of the production.

Until Belinda made her final exit.

I now regret that I was paying more attention to Sam and Jason at the time. But all Belinda was doing was walking off-stage, so it wasn't like I needed to focus on her. My other actors were ramping up to the big finish—and the bigger kiss. I was busy worrying about how we were going to do it with Eric sitting behind me, literally breathing down my neck. That boy has some hot breath. But even though I missed Belinda's mistake, Hope made sure we all knew about it.

And the tensions of the week finally exploded.

"Stage left!" Hope yelled out, causing Gary and me to jump in our seats. She was up on her feet, throwing down the script she'd been using to follow along. "Belinda, you just exited through the kitchen! Can't you do anything right?"

"Like it matters!" Alexis yelled before I could even react. "There's no kitchen back there. Besides, it's stupid that the kitchen is right next to the bedroom and living room anyway. Shouldn't there be like a dining room and stuff?" This coming from the girl living in a house with over two dozen rooms.

"What are you even doing here?" Hope asked. "Is the hair design that much of a challenge you need to be here *every* day?"

"We could ask the same about the playwriting," Holly added. "Isn't your job like done? Or do you think your play sucks so much that you have to be around every minute to fix it?"

"ENOUGH!" Sam yelled. "Can we please finish so we can go home before we're supposed to be back here?"

She was glaring at me like it was my fault. Like I had any control over the half dozen people that sat in on my rehearsals. The half dozen people that included her boyfriend and his shadow. That I hadn't invited in the first place.

"Fine," I said, standing. I needed to move. How was I supposed to direct with all these stupid distractions? "Belinda, can we take it from your exit again?"

"Excuse me?" she asked, like she hadn't heard me. She seemed to be occupied with her hands, which she was nervously wringing like Lady Macbeth and her damned spot. The brief outburst had clearly shaken her. Hope's continued huffing wasn't helping. Neither were the strained whispers coming from Alexis and Holly.

"Your exit," I said gently. I couldn't believe I was feeling sorry for Belinda. But she looked so lost up there onstage. Living with Hope and Alexis could not be fun. Hence the hand-wringing. It didn't seem like a new habit.

"Okay," she said. "Sorry."

Belinda gave her final line, then exited in the correct direction as Sam and Jason continued the scene. There was so much tension in the air, they were basically just reading lines to get to the end. It wasn't like there was any acting going on. Then again, it wasn't like there was any directing going on either.

"That's good for today," I said the moment before they

went in for the big kiss. I could see Eric out of the corner of my eye. He was intently leaning over the chair in front of him. As if waiting for his chance at an outburst. I figured we could work on the kiss later. The last thing any of us needed was more awkwardness. "Everybody go home."

Assorted grumbles filled the auditorium as the cast came down from the stage to collect their things. Belinda barely made it to the first row before her sister handed over her bags and Holly grabbed her and pulled her out of Hall Hall. I could tell that she'd wanted to say something to me, but they never gave her the chance. It was just as well, because Hope *was* making her way to me.

Not that I gave her the chance. "I'll meet you at Electra," I said, cutting her off. I was sure that I'd be hearing more than enough from her on the ride home.

Not that I expected Hope to go quietly. Thankfully, Sam, Eric, and Drew were there to head her off. They marched her up the aisle before she could attack, leaving Gary and me to break down the set.

"Let's get this done so we can get out of here," I said as we climbed up onto the stage.

"Are you okay?" he asked as we started pushing the assorted chairs and such backstage. We hadn't moved the real set pieces out of storage yet. It was just as well, because that would have taken longer to break down and I was so ready to leave.

"I just . . . I don't know what to do about Hope," I said. "She hates that I cast Belinda in this play. And she is going to keep blowing every mistake out of proportion."

"Can't you talk to her about it?"

"Talk to Hope? About her stepsisters?"

He shrugged like it wasn't the craziest suggestion in the entire world.

"Never tried," I said. "That's one subject I'm too afraid to approach. Much like the other powder keg that's getting ready to blow."

"You mean Eric?" Gary asked as he slid the final chair stage right.

"Sam doesn't even see what's coming," I said. "I can tell. And if I try to say something to her, she won't even hear it."

"So what are you going to do?"

I considered the many options open to me. All of them seemed to end in my murder. "Pray that this planetary alignment goes horribly wrong, throwing the moon off its axis and sending it hurtling to the Earth, killing us all so I don't have to worry about the play anymore."

Gary took a moment to let that one sink in.

"Until then," he said brightly, "you want to grab some food before coming back for Stargazing Night?"

"We're ordering pizza," I said. "Everyone's meeting at my place at six."

"Everyone?" Gary asked.

"Sam and Hope," I clarified. "And Eric and Drew."

"But I thought you and Drew—"

"It's a package deal," I explained. "Wherever Eric goes, so goes Drew. Suze might come too. If you want to bring like Madison or anyone, that'd be okay."

"Oh . . . maybe," he said.

I grabbed my bag and slung it over my shoulder. "Later."

"Later," he said as I left the auditorium. I found Sam waiting for me by Electra. Since Sam lived in Santa Monica, it made little sense for her to go home and then come back. Especially since her mom was stuck at school setting up.

"Where's Hope?" I asked as I let her in to Electra.

"I asked Eric to take her home so she can cool off. She went a little crazy this afternoon."

"That she did," I agreed. "And Eric didn't have a problem spending five seconds away from you?"

She shrugged. "He was acting all huffy for some reason. Said he'd see us at your place later."

I wanted to thank her for confirming that she had no clue that he was a tad jealous over her role in the play, but seeing how that would require me to point out what she was missing, I thought it best to stay mum on the subject. Color me surprised to find that she was bringing it up on her own.

"You want to talk about it?" she asked.

"Talk about what?" I replied, bracing myself for a deep and meaningful conversation about how she should approach the end of the play without upsetting her boyfriend.

"Hope," she said.

Oh.

Never mind.

"Not really," I said as I started up Electra, listening for the engine to catch. It did, which is always cause for a minor celebration because the car is, like, three times my age.

"You know she's got issues," Sam said, heedless of my desire to avoid the subject. Or the issues that were coming her way.

"Look, Sam," I said. "You're my best friend, but you're also my lead actress. I can't talk to you about this."

"That's stupid," she said.

"Would you go to Mr. Randall complaining about Jason if he did something to annoy you during a show?"

She stopped to think about the question as I pulled out of the parking lot. "I'll give you that," she finally said. "But if it gets so crazy that you need to talk . . ."

"You'll be the first person I come to," I assured her.

"You better," she said.

"I just hope we can get through tonight without another major incident," I said.

"We'll have Eric, Drew, and Suze to help keep things calm."

"And Gary," I said. "He's coming by the house for pizza too."

"Gary's coming?" Sam asked in a non-nonchalant way. Which is to say, she was fishing for information.

"Um . . . yeah," I said. "Back when we planned to go furniture shopping, he asked about tagging along to Stargazing Night."

"He said he wanted to tag along?" Sam asked. "He used those words?"

"Well, I don't think he knew it was a group outing," I clarified. "He asked if I wanted to go with him."

Sam burst out with a laugh. "You idiot!"

Her calling me names was nothing new, so I went with it. "What did I do now?"

She shook her head in resignation. "He was asking you on a date."

"What?" I nearly veered off the road.

"Smooth," Sam said, steadying the wheel for me.

"He wasn't asking me on a date," I said. "He's my associate stage manager."

"What's that got to do with anything?"

"He's never said he was gay," I said.

"Technically, neither have you," she said, laughing some more.

"It's not a date," I protested. "We were going to run an errand. It was convenient." The laughter continued. "How was I supposed to know?" I mean, *honestly*. When a guy asks a girl out to Stargazing Night, it's pretty clear that romance is the goal. Or, if not romance, something that could pass for romance in a high school setting. Is it my fault I had no experience with guys asking me . . . to do anything? This is the problem with having mostly female friends. It distorts your perspective on dealing with guys.

Oddly, I'd found myself in a similar situation over the summer when I realized I was on some kind of pseudodate with Sam's Gay Best Friend, Marq. Here I was about to embark on what could arguably be considered my second real date, and once again, it caught me totally off guard.

I really need to be more observant.

Starlight Express

"We are not talking about it," Hope said before she would step into my kitchen. "I have finally calmed down. I am dealing with the fact that you refuse to listen to me about how Belinda is going to ruin my play. I am coping with how you insist on going along like nothing is wrong. Like everything is fine. I am waiting for all hell to break loose. But until that time, I intend to relax and enjoy life. Make the most out of Stargazing Night. Maybe even make contact with an alien race."

For someone who started off her monologue by saying "we are not talking about it," Hope was sure having a problem shutting up. Wait. She wasn't done.

"But we will not discuss the play. The cast. The inherent problems. Or any of it," she said as she finally took that step inside. "Because we *totally* have to talk about you going on your very first date!"

I slowly turned to my so-called best friend Sam. "I was wondering what took you so long in the bathroom. You snuck into my room and called her, didn't you?"

"This is too momentous an occasion for me to go through alone," Sam said. "I need to share it with someone who truly appreciates the milestone."

"You need to share it with someone who will make fun of me mercilessly until Gary shows up at the door," I corrected her.

Sam smiled a not-so-innocent smile. "What makes you think we're going to stop when he gets here?"

"You're not wearing *that?*" Hope asked, giving me the once-over.

I looked fine in my T-shirt, jeans, and fedora. I'd been wearing the outfit all day and nobody said anything about it earlier. But as Sam and Hope led me to my bedroom, they explained all the reasons why that wasn't necessarily a good thing. I doubted that Gary was going to go home and change for a school function, but they insisted that I should.

Which is when the fun began.

And by "fun" I mean "hell."

"How's this?" I asked a half hour later as I came back from the bathroom. I was modeling the *fifth* outfit they'd insisted I try on for them. Outfits one through four made me look either too skinny, too pale, too dorky, or even (you guessed it) too gay. Funny how my wardrobe never said so much about me *before*.

"Lose the fedora," Hope said. "It looks costumey." Says the girl dressed in a black riding outfit with pink leather boots and matching pink contacts. (Just because the Headmaster said we weren't supposed to be in costume, didn't mean Hope was going to listen. As wacky as the ensemble was, it was also something we could see her normally wearing to school.)

But back to me . . . we all knew that the fedora wasn't going anywhere. It was the equivalent of Linus's blue blanket, and I was not taking it off. Besides, it went great with the vintage jeans, vintage T-shirt, and vintage blazer I was wearing. So I didn't look like a walking vintage store, I was wearing modern sneakers, but they had a classic style I could get away with.

"Perfect!" Sam announced, springing off the bed. "Just one thing." She slipped an origami flower that she'd made out of a page from *Entertainment Weekly* into the lapel. "Now it's even more perfect."

I checked myself out in the mirror, liking what I saw. "This I can do."

"Still think you should lose the fedora," Hope muttered.

I let it go. We'd been getting along well since her announcement that we weren't going to discuss what we weren't going to discuss. This probably had to do with how much fun she and Sam were having over my utter mortification that I'd accepted a date without realizing it. I'd hardly had the chance to wonder if I actually wanted to go on this date with Gary.

On paper he is a pretty good match. Funny. Cute. Stylish but not a slave to fashion. Loves theater. Maybe a little on the geeky side. And, okay, he's a junior, but there's nothing wrong with younger guys. The only issue was that I wasn't so sure I felt *that way* about him.

To be fair, I had never thought of him in *that way*. As it's been established, I didn't realize he was asking me on a date when he asked me on a date. If I had known at the time, I'm not sure how I would have reacted. I imagine there would have been some shock followed by stammering. And maybe some cold sweat. But how would I have answered? Was it fair to let him go on thinking it was a date when I wasn't sure I wanted to date him? Then again, we were going to have a half dozen people along for the ride, so I doubted there was going to be much date-type activity.

I also doubted the whole origami flower accessory and removed it from my lapel. Sam merely shrugged, taking no offense.

"You calmed down yet?" Hope asked.

"I was never not calm," I lied in the form of a double negative.

"Good," she said, "because I can't do this anymore. We have *got* to talk about Belinda."

Suddenly . . . not so calm.

I shot a forlorn glance to the hallway. Should have known she'd break her own rule. At least she seemed calmer than she'd been during rehearsal. Not that that was going to stop me from delaying the conversation. "Everyone's going to be here soon."

"I can bitch while we move to the kitchen."

Of that I had no doubt.

"I still think you should use the revised play," Hope said.

"The original works fine for me," I replied.

"How would you know if you don't even look at other one?"

"I looked," I said. Okay. I admit it. In a weak moment, I did consider changing plays. It's not that Belinda wasn't doing okay, because she was. It's just, beside Sam and Jason—two of the best actors in school history—"okay" isn't quite good enough.

Sam, however, seemed disappointed in me for humoring Hope. Not that I did it to humor her. I was mainly trying to deal with my own insecurities. Insecurities that were not helped by Sam's lack of support.

"You're lying," Hope said.

"I looked! And even if I was going to change scripts, I couldn't even begin to consider yours. Belinda's character is only on two pages."

"No," Hope insisted. "She's *in* a full half of the play. She only *speaks* for two pages."

"We don't need to change scripts," Sam said.

"Well, we need to do something," Hope said.

"Need to do what?" Blaine asked from behind the refrigerator door.

"Don't you have a home?" I asked. "You're always here."

"I'm here because if I didn't cook for you guys while your dad was away, you and your mom would starve."

I couldn't argue with that one. "No need to put on the chef's hat tonight. We're ordering pizza. I'm thinking Hawaiian style. Who's with me?

"No changing the subject," Hope said. "*Belimia* needs work."

"I know she does," I said. "And I intend to work with her."

"Belimia?" Blaine asked while he sniffed the milk and generally checked the expiration dates on the contents of the fridge for Mom and me.

"That's what we call Belinda sometimes," I explained. That or any derivation of an eating disorder. She and Alexis are frighteningly thin.

"This is Hope's sister we're talking about?" Blaine asked.

"*Step*sister," we all said.

"And we suspect that she has an eating disorder?" Blaine asked.

"Her and Alerexia put together don't even weigh as much as a pre-baby-weight Nicole Richie," I said, picking some shredded chicken out of a container that was sitting on the counter. I wondered if it was still within its freshness date.

"So rather than do something to help someone you think has a serious eating disorder—like talking to Hope's parents—you make fun of these girls? Is that what we're saying?"

All three of us stood there speechless. To be honest, it was kind of a rhetorical question. I mean, we didn't *really* think that Belinda and Alexis were . . . well, we did, but we didn't believe it was like . . . serious.

"Just some food for thought," Blaine said, taking a bite out of an apple before he took the chicken from my hand, threw out the container, and left us to feel like idiots as he went to join my mom in her studio.

"Okay, um," Sam said. "That aside. Hope, Belinda's doing fine for someone who just started acting."

"Which brings us back to the question at hand," Hope said.

I braced myself. "Which is?"

"Why in the world did you cast someone with no experience in my play?" she asked. She wasn't yelling. She didn't even seem angry. If anything, she was kind of . . . sad. "You know how important this is. I never show my work to anyone. *Anyone*. And not only did you cast one of the people I hate most in the world to be in the play but you won't even listen to me about it."

I wanted to point out that I had listened, I simply didn't do anything about it. But I wasn't sure that would go over so well. I got what Hope was saying. From her perspective, I could even understand why she was upset. But she was letting her emotions get in the way of reality. The play wasn't nearly as bad as she was making it out to be. Some might say it wasn't bad at all.

Mind you, I wasn't about to say it to her. And thankfully I didn't have to. A knock at the kitchen door saved us all from the rest of the conversation.

Eric and Drew entered without waiting for me to open the door for them. I'd say it was rude, but considering there was a big glass window between us and them, they could easily see us standing in the kitchen. It wasn't like they were going to walk in on anything.

Once Eric was inside, he walked right up to Sam and gave her the most intense kiss I'd ever seen him plant on her lips. I couldn't help suspecting that it had more to do with the final scene of our play than any genuine feelings of romance overwhelming him at the moment. Kind of a marking-his-territory thing. Like when dogs pee on each other. Well, you know what I mean. The kiss continued to a point where the other three people in the room were starting to get uncomfortable.

His territory was getting thoroughly marked even though no one in the immediate vicinity was exactly interested.

"Anyone else hungry?" Drew asked. He seemed to be directing the question to Hope, not me. "I could go for a white pizza."

"We can't order yet," I said. Then I quickly added, "Suze isn't here yet. It would be rude. Not to wait. For everyone, I mean."

Smooth.

When Eric finally let Sam up for air she had to go and add, "Bryan's date isn't here yet either."

"Date?" Eric asked with too much enthusiasm and *way* too much volume. Thankfully, my mom's studio was soundproof.

"It's not a date," I said. "It's just . . . Gary's coming with us." I glanced Drew's way to see if there was a reaction. There was. He was rearranging the refrigerator magnets. The activity was quite attention-consuming, considering we only had two magnets.

"No," Hope said. "Gary's going with you. I doubt he knew the rest of us were coming along."

"Hey, man," Eric said. "We can go on ahead if you two want to be alone." Considering Eric's mom is with another woman, it wasn't surprising that he was on the bandwagon. I never expected him to be leading the parade, though.

"What about the pizza?" Drew asked.

Hope smacked him, saving me the trouble. Not that I would have hit him. But I wanted to.

"Stay," I said. I wasn't being polite. I didn't want to be alone with Gary. Which is odd, as I'd been alone with him a few times in the past week and never gave it a second thought. But suddenly I was giving it second, third, and fourth thoughts. Then again, maybe there would have been less thinking going on if I had let Drew run on ahead like a good little boy.

But all thinking ceased when the front doorbell rang.

"Oh, shit," I said, realizing that the bell also rang in Mom's studio . . . where Blaine was. The last thing I needed was him answering the door. Blaine can be extra sensitive to the things in my life I'm not ready to let him know. He would have way too much fun with the news that I was going on a date.

I bolted out of the kitchen, yelling, "I got it!" loud enough that I figured it had to pierce through the soundproofing. I knew it wasn't Suze at the door. My close friends know to go to the kitchen door when they come over. It's the more direct route into the part of the house where we usually hang, and it avoids having to cross through the museumlike rooms that Mom pays someone to keep in pristine condition. But Gary wouldn't do anything like that. He's only been to my house once, or maybe twice, before.

I stopped a few strides short of the front door to compose myself and check my reflection in the hall mirror. I straightened my jacket and tipped my fedora in a casual manner. Didn't want to seem too eager. I thought about taking off the jacket and flinging it over my shoulder, but that was *too* casual. When snickering sounds coming from behind my back alerted me that I had an audience, I gave up on the mirror and quickly threw open the door. Gary was about to press the bell again. Guess I was taking a tad longer than I'd thought.

"You're here!" I stated the obvious.

"And many other things," he said, a comment I wasn't entirely sure how to take.

"Come in," I said, taking the next logical step in our conversation. Considering how he was looking over my shoulder, I assumed our audience wasn't being as discreet as I'd hoped they would be. "As you can probably see, the gang's all here . . . well, except Suze."

He leaned toward me and whispered, "Why are they hiding behind a potted plant?"

"It's fake," I said, like that explained anything or was even the answer to his question.

He nodded as if he understood completely . . . which made one of us who did.

Seeing how we now outnumbered the chairs in the kitchen, I told my friends to come out from their (lack of) hiding place, and we convened in the living room. There was some awkward shifting of seats while Sam and Hope tried to navigate it so that I could sit with Gary. They were about as subtle as when Danny Kaye does the same thing in *White Christmas*. (*Aside:* Yes, it may be an obscure reference, but if you know what I'm talking about, you know what I'm talking about. If not, rent the film and pay attention every time the redheaded guy goes, "Boy-girl-boy-girl.") Seeing how we had twice the number of boys to girls, I wound up seated on the couch between Gary and Drew.

My friends and I weren't usually at a loss for things to talk about. And Gary wasn't exactly known for being shy. Yet, as we all sat in my living room, the conversation wasn't exactly flowing.

"So," I said to Gary. "Looking forward to Stargazing Night?" What? Like I was going to start talking about the play with Hope in the room?

"Not really," Gary said. "After the last one, when all we saw was some space dust."

"Yeah," I said. "Boring."

Scintillating discussion, isn't it?

We're both usually much more interesting, but I suspect we were suffering from performance anxiety seeing how our date was being acted out in front of a live audience.

"Hello!" Suze called from the kitchen.

Never in my life have I seen a group of people jump up from their seats faster.

Relief washed over us as we greeted our friend, way warmly, and began an in-depth discussion on the size, quantity, and topping choices of the pizzas we would order. We finally settled on one veggie, one meat lover's, and one plain pie for the nine of us (adults included) before settling in to awkward silence again.

This one was salvaged by Blaine, who joined us and filled the many conversational gaps with a fascinating lecture on the dog toy industry and the introduction of eco-friendly chew toys in recent years. Okay, "fascinating" might be a bit of an exaggeration, but the topic carried us right through the arrival and consumption of the pizza and got us to the point where we could leave for the event without being the first to arrive.

Eric had secured his dad's mondo SUV, which was twice the gas-guzzling size of Eric's own SUV, so we could ride to school together. Sam and Hope subjected us to the same forced assigned seating that once again found me squeezed between Gary and Drew. Seeing how Drew easily could have shared the back bench with Hope and Suze, I wondered what it meant that he kept finding his way beside me.

"Should we sing road trip songs?" Gary asked as we set off. He was joking, of course.

The ride to school was on the path to discomfortville again when Gary introduced a subject that we could all participate in.

"Where are you applying?" he asked me.

"UCLA and USC!" I replied with way more enthusiasm than this topic usually inspires. "Probably for film. Maybe for directing. Not sure about that."

"You're not planning on hitting the road as soon as you graduate?"

"And leave L.A.? What would be the point?"

"I keep telling him we should backpack through Europe first," Sam chimed in from the front.

"And I keep telling her we should stay in five-star hotels

across Europe," I replied. Not that either of us could afford it.

"I'm in," Eric added, even though no one had extended an invitation. Although, *he* could afford it. If only there was a way to convince myself that I'd enjoy spending a summer traveling with Eric. Of course, then there was a chance Drew might come along.

"What about you, Sam?" Gary asked Sam.

"UCLA," she replied. "Unless someone offers me a scholarship. Then I'll go anywhere they want me to."

"Good luck at the University of Siberia," I said to her before turning to Gary. "I hear they have an intensive drama program."

"Because it's too cold there to ever leave the theater," he replied, playing along.

"Indubitably."

"Are you ever going to talk to me about the painting?" Drew asked me in an abrupt subject switch. Needless to say, this caught me quite off guard. I'd been putting off the conversation about the art project for *Achromantic* for a week. Not for any specific reason, really. It's just that every time Drew was around, he acted like I was the last person in the world he wanted to talk to. In my defense, he didn't come up to me to talk about it either.

Except, I suppose he just did.

"Sorry," I said. "I've been busy."

"So I noticed."

Wow. There were many ways I could take that comment. And I took it every way possible. "I said, *sorry*."

"If I want to include this in my portfolio for college apps, I've got to get it done soon."

"I didn't realize you were applying . . . you have a portfolio?"

"Not much of one," he said. "Which is why I need to get working on the painting. Besides, I assume you want to have it done in time for opening night."

"Well . . . um . . . yes," I said, noticing that the college conversation around me had stopped and we seemed to be the center of attention. "Let's talk tomorrow. At lunch."

"I'm not in school tomorrow," he said. "My dad has booked me on my twelfth college tour of the fall."

"You've visited eleven colleges?" I asked.

"On the West Coast alone," he said. It's not that Drew's parents are strict or obsessive or demanding or any of that stuff. They're just very, *very* enthusiastic about education.

"Okay," I said. "Friday. Lunch. You and me. In the art room."

"Finally," Drew said, and turned to look out the window, dropping the matter.

I turned back to my date. "Drew and I are going to work on the painting Friday," I said, for some reason feeling the need to explain myself. "For the play."

"Yeah," he said. "I heard."

Dark of the Moon

We pulled up to school a few minutes of stilted
conversation later. We'd arrived early enough to fit the SUV
into one of the larger spots in the back row, but the place was
filling quickly. Stargazing Night is a big deal at Orion. There
aren't many high schools with a full-on observatory on campus. Not that our founders had foreseen some great need for
the scientific education of the teens in Malibu. We'd inherited
the building from the scientific college our campus used to be.
The residents of the area would have much preferred it if the
original owners had bulldozed the area so there could be
unobstructed views of the ocean. But we all went along with
the charade that it was a great community-building event as
the locals walked the winding road to school and joined us in
an evening of polite hostility.

Much like high school itself.

There's only one telescope, so the line to view this

unprecedented planetary phenomenon was already kind of long. And please don't think I'm making light of scientific exploration when I don't tell you what we were all there to see. It's that, in the scramble to create another stellar (ha) event for Orion Academy to show off with, no one had bothered to explain what we were there to see. Oh, I'm sure the science teachers had mentioned it in all their classes, but between putting together a show and getting the college application process under way, most of us had been too preoccupied to realize that there was education going on during the day.

Let alone the stuff we were now expected to learn at night.

"What should we do first?" Eric asked, pointing to the sign that directed guests to the various events. Since standing in line for an hour isn't all that fun, Headmaster Collins makes it into a party, with glow lights and science exhibits and space-themed catering. The classic moon pies are to die for, but I recommend avoiding the freeze-dried ice cream. "Should we hit the moon bounce, the moonbeam, or the moon river?"

That headmaster is so creative with his themes, isn't he?

"Well, we're too big for the moon bounce," Sam said.

"The moonbeam is like the lamest light show around," Hope added. "It's a couple teachers pointing colored flashlights at a wall."

"And the moon river is just a toy sailboat in the school fountain," Jason said as he joined our ever expanding group. "What took you guys so long?" Although he addressed the comment to us "guys," he was focusing all his attention directly at Sam.

This? Was not a good development.

It was also something that did not go unnoticed by others. Particularly Eric, who—I kid you not—threw his arm around Sam's shoulders in a move that clearly claimed her as his. Normally I would make fun of such an action for its ridiculousness, but I was kind of on Eric's side on this one. Largely because I didn't need the potential scandal disrupting my show.

Of course, all of this came out of a simple greeting, so Eric and I could have been overreacting.

"I told you we'd be here after seven," Sam replied.

Or maybe we weren't.

"Jason's hanging with us?" Eric asked with not even barely contained jealousy.

"The more the merrier," Hope said, threading her arm into Jason's in a move that was so smooth I almost applauded it. I'd have wrapped my own arm around him too, but I didn't want him to get the wrong idea. Or my date to get jealous.

"Mom's working the glowing-junk booth," Sam said, directing us to our first activity of the evening.

"Glowing junk?" I asked. "Is that the formal name of the booth?"

"Come on," Sam said with an exasperated moan. Most people would direct their friends as far away from their mom as possible at these kinds of things, especially if their mom was also a teacher at the school. Not Sam. Aside from being one of the most popular teachers at school, Anne is one of the best moms (besides my own mom, of course).

We saw the booth long before we got there, largely because of the whole glowing-junk aspect. Red, green, blue, and orange glow sticks and necklaces and things I couldn't even identify lit up the night. The only thing that was missing was some glow-in-the-dark dog toys.

"Thank God you're here!" Anne said in an unusually warm greeting upon seeing her daughter. "Headmaster Collins has been running us around like crazy since school let out. I have *got* to go to the bathroom. Work the table for me, will you?"

"Good to see you too, Mom," Sam said, taking a position by the cash box.

"I *looooove* you," Anne said as she gave her daughter a big wet kiss. "And Bryan—"

"I love you too," I said.

"Well, yes," she said. "But that wasn't what I was going to say." Oh. "I've got an extra box of glowing junk in my classroom and I need a big, strong man to carry it out for me."

I looked at the big, strong men surrounding me and wondered why she was telling me this. I raised my eyebrows at her, letting them say everything that needed to be said.

"I'll go," Jason offered, picking up on the language of my eyebrows.

I saluted him and sent them on their merry way.

When they were barely out of hearing range, Eric burst out, "I don't want you kissing him!"

The glow from the junk in the booth perfectly captured

shocked reactions on all our faces, and most notably on Eric's. I can only assume he hadn't meant to say that out loud.

"I wasn't planning on it," Sam said.

"Not now," he said. "In the show. I don't want you kissing Jason."

The rest of us got very busy examining all the glowing junk around us. It was just amazing the things they could do with toxic glowing liquids these days.

As Sam's director I wondered if it was my place to jump in and explain how the kiss is integral to the plot and all that. I could have given Eric a detailed explanation of the dramatic process and how a kiss between two actors means nothing. I could have reassured him that it would be staged in such a way that Sam and Jason's lips wouldn't even have to touch. I could have done all those things, but it should come as no surprise that I did not do any of them.

Besides, I never had the chance. Holly and the Hollettes sauntered up to us, disrupting any potential defense that I never would have made in the first place.

"About time you got here," Holly said.

Never have I been so popular in my entire life. This directing thing sure elevated my status at school. Unfortunately.

"What do you want?" Hope intervened, with all the attitude you can wring out of that question.

"I want you to stop throwing your considerable weight around and give Belinda a chance to act," Holly said, getting right to business.

"*Give* her a chance?" Hope asked. "That's what we've been waiting for."

For some reason Holly then turned to me. "Just because you suck up to Mr. Randall so he lets you direct in the festival doesn't mean you can do whatever you want."

How did this turn on me? "What'd I do?"

"What *haven't* you done?" Holly asked. "Put her in Hope's play. Barely spend any time working with her because you're so busy fawning all over your friends. Don't stand up for her when Hope flips out. You are such an ass!"

Ass? Me? I've been called many things in my life—some of them quite creative, actually; kids can be imaginative when it comes to cutting down others—but no one had ever called me an ass before and meant it. What it lacked in style, it made up for in cutting right to the heart of things. And, okay, sure . . . when she put it like that it certainly made me out to be kind of assy, but she was totally taking things out of context.

"Look, I—"

"What did I miss now?" Anne asked, bringing some much-needed lightness to the proceedings. And literal lightness since Jason was accompanying her with a box of glowing junk.

I swear, Anne's got momdar or something. She has this impeccable way of honing in on trouble brewing between us and them and making sure she's around to head it off. I only wish her timing was a little better. She always comes in a couple seconds too late.

"We were talking about the play," Belinda said meekly.

"And how your daughter's clique is treating Belle so horribly," Holly said.

Wait. We're a clique? How come nobody told me?

I'm in a clique.

"I don't know that Stargazing Night is the proper place for this discussion," Anne said. "And if Belinda has a problem with the play, it would be more appropriate for her to take it up with her director." Great. *More* pressure. "And if that fails to resolve the issue, Mr. Randall is the faculty adviser for the drama students, so the matter should be brought to his attention." I saw no need for Anne to go telling them to rat me out to Mr. Randall.

Holly was not satisfied with that course of action, which is understandable. She's used to an immediate response to her complaints. Her father pays good money for that kind of reaction. "I don't—"

But Anne was used to dealing with the Mayflowers. "Either way, I'm certain that Belinda is more than capable of handling the issue herself, much as I'm sure she appreciates having a friend like you come to her aid."

With no way to respond to that, Holly and her minions walked away, leaving silence in their wake.

"I could use some air," I said to Gary.

"Sounds like a plan," he agreed, not bothering to mention that we were already outside.

We excused ourselves from the group before any other drama could occur. On the bright side, Holly's cameo had put a halt to Eric's tirade over the kiss. With Anne back, and Jason too, I was pretty sure that conversation had been put on hold. As Gary and I walked off, I made the mistake of looking back to check that everyone was behaving and saw that, for the first time in forever, Drew wasn't occupied with examining his footwear. He was watching us walk away.

Gary's hand brushed against mine, bringing me back to the guy I was actually with as opposed to the one I'd left behind. I couldn't tell if this was an accident or a signal. Did he want to hold hands? At a public event? Or was he just walking too close. I thought about brushing his hand as well. Or maybe just grabbing it and holding it in mine. But I could have been wrong about the whole thing. Maybe he just wanted to be friends. Maybe Sam and Hope had convinced me something was there when really nothing was. Maybe he was totally straight and secretly in love with his best friend who had just sprang out of the bushes in front of us.

"Hey!" Madison Wu said. Some random junior guy was following her out of those bushes. He was somewhat disheveled and she didn't even look embarrassed by it at all. "Fancy running into you two here." She laughed way harder than necessary, in my opinion.

"Maddie!" Gary said, giving her a hug. "I was wondering where you were sneaking around. And with who." Gary scanned the guy up and down in much the way I tend to look over any guy that shows interest in Hope or Sam.

"The bushes are unoccupied now," Maddie said.

Even in the darkness I could see Gary blush. "That's okay," he said. "We were heading to the bluff."

"Even better," Madison said with a wink.

I would have to be an idiot not to catch those signs. My suspicions were officially confirmed.

"We're going to go before you make this even more uncomfortable," Gary said, grabbing my arm and pulling me away from his best friend. It wasn't quite holding my hand, but it was more intimate than most guys usually got with me.

"Sorry about that," Gary said.

"I'm the last person you need to apologize to for the behavior of your female friends," I said. "In case you haven't noticed, mine tend to be overwhelming in many of the same ways."

"Yeah," he said. "It's like she wants to be my sister, best friend, mom, and boss all at the same time."

"Multiply that by two and you have my relationship with Sam and Hope," I said.

"Oh, God," he said. "I can't imagine Madison times two. It's bad enough she keeps making this night into such a . . ." He trailed off when he realized where the rest of his sentence was going to lead him.

Since he was bold enough to ask me out, I figured I might as well be the one to get everything out in the open. "So this is a date?"

We'd reached the bluff. By the reaction on his face to my question, I was afraid he was going to jump.

"If you want it to be," he said. "But if you'd rather hang out with your—"

"No!" I said. "I mean, yes . . . well . . . I don't know." There were so many things running through my head and there was a lot I didn't know. "When you asked me . . . no one's asked me out before. Not officially. I didn't know you meant it that way. So I just assumed . . ." There I was making assumptions again. "And then when Sam and Hope told me it was a date—"

"Your friends *told* you?" he asked amid heavy laughter. "Man, we really do let our female friends control too much of our lives."

"Too true," I said, laughing along.

Once the laughter ended, Gary asked the question I'd been dreading. "How did you feel then? When they told you that I'd asked you out."

"Confused."

"I hear that," he said. "And now?"

I thought about it some more. "I'm still going with confused."

"Fair enough," he said, though he did take a step away from me.

"It's not . . ." I said, not sure where I was going. Like Sam's GBF, Marq, I had another great guy presenting himself to me, all for the taking. Do you know how rare that is in a high school setting? Even for the straight kids! And yet . . . "There's so much going on right now, with the play and everything," I said. "And you're my associate stage manager. Which kind of makes me your boss. Think of the scandal."

"Good point," he said, even though I'd been making a joke. "Really?"

"You know how everyone at this stupid school is just

waiting for everyone else to fail," he said. "Imagine if anything goes wrong with the play—"

"Which it won't," I quickly said, hoping to avoid the jinx.

"Which it definitely won't," he agreed. "But if the unimag-
inable happens and something does go wrong, everyone's
going to say it's my fault for distracting you."

I wanted to argue the point, but I'd been at Orion longer
than he had and was pretty sure he was on the right track with
this one.

"So you're going to let me get away with the 'I'm your boss'
excuse?"

"For now," he said. "It's only a week and a half until the
show goes up. Then you're fair game."

I nodded. "I guess I am." Surely I'd know by then if I wanted
to go out with Gary. Right?

"This is going to be some cast party," he added with a mischievous grin.

Have to say that I was incredibly flattered to be the cause
of that mischievous grin.

It truly was the perfect moment. Us standing there on the
bluff, being mostly honest with each other. If it were a play
Hope had written, this would be the part where we kissed. All
I had to do was lean forward and let him know I was willing.

But I didn't.

And I soon came to regret it.

"We should get back before people start talking," Gary
said.

"Oh, *that* happened the moment we got out of Eric's SUV

together," I said. "Congratulations, by the way. You're officially out of the closet."

"Thanks," he said with a comically confused look on his
face. Believe me, I knew the feeling well.

"So," he said, using the universally accepted word for
changing subjects. "If you don't mind me asking . . . what *are*
you going to do about the tension during rehearsals?"

"I have to do something, don't I?"

Gary shrugged, but it was one of those shrugs that kind of
implied that the answer was "yes, you idiot." Well, the "idiot"
part may not have been there. "Why is Hope *so* mad at
Belinda?" he asked.

"Honestly," I said. "She's never shared. All I know is
Hope has been deep in a feud with the steps for years.
When she and I became friends I kind of had to hate them
by association."

"Ah," he said knowingly. "The enemy of my best friend is
my enemy. Been there. But why is Hope taking it out on the
play? Belinda is perfect."

"Perfect?" I asked speaking through my stupid director's
mouth. "I wouldn't say *perfect*. We do have to work on the
chicken necking thing. And truthfully, Belinda isn't at Sam
and Jason's level—"

There was a "but" coming. I swear it! *But* I never had the
chance to get it out because we walked right into the subject of our conversation. Belinda was standing in the middle
of the path as we turned a corner heading back to campus.
Clearly she had heard what I was saying. The tears welling

in her eyes told me that much. Even though she totally played it off.

"I was looking for you," she said. "To apologize. For Holly. She had no right to attack you like that."

"Thanks," I said. "It's—"

"No," Belinda said. "I get it. And I know Hope wrote a new version of the play. I saw it at the house." I tried not to think that Hope left it out for her to see. "If you want to use it, I won't make a big deal or anything."

"*But*—" I finally got out.

But she held up a hand to stop me. "It's okay. I understand."

She ran off before I could say anything else.

Okay, that was a lie. I could have said many things. Many, *many* things. I could have grabbed her. Called out to her. Explained what I'd meant. Told her how good I honestly thought she was. Finished the damn sentence: "*but* nobody in this school is at the level of Sam and Jason."

I did none of that.

Because apparently I am an ass.

The Servant of Two Masters

Gary was placing the chairs in the center of Anne's room to match our set design when I interrupted, handing him a piece of paper. "Here. Put this on the door, please."

He stopped what he was doing and read what I had printed out when I'd gotten home from Stargazing Night. "Are you serious?"

"Yes," I said. "And it's long past due."

Nothing major had happened the rest of the night. The lingering tensions had been obvious in almost every member of our group when Gary and I got back from the bluff. You could tell by how nobody immediately pulled me aside to ask me what went on with Gary and me. Oh, that happened later, but if my friends had been in a better mood, they would have pounced as soon as they had a chance. Sam and Hope were disappointed to hear there was no boy-on-boy lip action but didn't give me nearly the amount of grief they should have. Which was another sign something needed to be done.

"Some people are not going to like this," he said.

"I don't care," I said. "I should have done it from the start. Now please get it up before anyone gets here."

"Gladly," he said. There was almost a skip in his step as he grabbed the tape from Anne's desk and made his way to the door. His response was enough to confirm that I was doing the right thing. "It's up," he said as he came back into the room, shutting the door behind him. "Let's hope it works."

"Thanks for the optimism," I said, knowing he was right. An eight-and-a-half-by-eleven-inch piece of paper with some writing on it wasn't going to do anything if people just ignored it. Then the responsibility would fall on me.

The paper got its first test less than a minute later.

"What's this?" Sam asked, pointing to the sign as she opened the door. Eric was standing behind her out in the hall. So far it was doing its job.

"It is what it says it is," I replied.

"'Closed Rehearsal,'" she read. "Since when?"

"Since we should have been doing that from day one," I explained. "I'm sorry, but we've only got a little over a week to pull this all together. We don't need distractions."

"So I'm a distraction?" Eric asked from the hall. His tone was playful, with maybe a touch of seriousness.

"Only the best kind, honey," she replied, pouring it on. Sam must have agreed, because she stepped back into the hall, whispered some sweet nothings, gave Eric a kiss, and sent him on his way.

So far so good.

Jason came in a moment later, entourage-free as usual. If only all actors could be like Jason. He'd given me nothing but his best, most conflict-free work since I'd put him in the cast. Okay, sure, the mere existence of him in the play was causing some of the Sam/Eric stress, but that wasn't Jason's fault.

We hit the first real snag right after that when Belinda showed up with Alexis in tow.

"What the hell's this supposed to mean?"

I'll give you one guess who said that.

I ignored her.

"Hey, Belinda," I said as she came in with her bigmouthed sister following closely behind. "I hope you don't mind, but we're going to have a closed rehearsal today."

"Why?" Alexis asked. "Because Holly got on your case last night and you don't want me around now?"

Wow. It's rare that Alexis is ever right on two counts at the same time. I took off points because she was seeing it as a cause-and-effect thing. Like Holly got on my case and I'm punishing Alexis for it. That wasn't the case. Not entirely. Holly did get on my case about how my rehearsals were going. And she was—gulp—kind of right. But kicking Alexis to the curb was only a happy side effect of the main issue. I didn't want *anyone* sitting in and causing problems.

"Belinda, your guest would be welcome at Mr. Randall's

rehearsal," I said, still ignoring Alexis. "I understand that his cast would welcome help with their hair for the show."

Alexis *really* didn't like me bringing her so-called professionalism into this. "I was going to—"

"Alexis, please," Belinda said, pulling her sister aside. She spoke softly so we couldn't overhear . . . even though *I* could. "Let it go. I've got a lot of work—"

"I'm not going to leave you alone with these jerks," Alexis said, showing a surprising amount of sisterly concern. Even odder, I was apparently the bad guy in this equation. Did the world turn on its axis while I wasn't paying attention? Is that the unique planetary alignment we were supposed to be watching on Stargazing Night?

"I'll be fine," Belinda said. "Go mess up Holly's hair."

This suggestion made Alexis smile maliciously, reminding me of exactly who she is. She took off without another comment.

"Thanks," I said to Belinda before she could apologize to me for something else totally out of her control.

"Now that we're all here," I said to Gary, "please lock the door." I could have locked it myself, but I wanted to make it clear exactly what I was doing.

Sam even helped me out with that. "What about Hope?" she asked.

"The script is locked," I said to my cast, directing the comment to Belinda specifically. "It was locked before we had auditions. And it will remain locked. The playwright's services are no longer required." I turned to Gary. "The door."

There was no skip in his step this time as Gary walked over to the door and did as his director told him.

"Let's get this rehearsal started," I said.

The actors were settling in to opening positions when the expected knock came.

"Ignore it," I said to Belinda as she readied her first line.

The knock turned into a bang.

"She's not going to go away," Sam said.

I sighed. What Sam said was true. I couldn't let a locked door fight this battle. I owed it to my friend to do it to her face. "Take five," I said needlessly. I unlocked the door, opening it a crack but placing my foot at the bottom so that it would not open any wider than I wanted it to. I was under no illusion that Hope wouldn't slam the door into me, but it gave me a smidge more confidence.

"Why's the door locked?" Hope asked.

"I'm working with the actors today," I explained. "Trying to minimize the distractions."

"You're saying I'm a distraction?"

"You, Eric, Alexis, Holly," I said. "You're all distractions."

"Yeah, but I'm your friend," she reminded me. "And I wrote the play."

"Right now I'm choosing to be the director of your play. And as your director *and* your friend, it is in the best interest of your play that we have a closed rehearsal."

"I disagree," she said, her anger rising.

"Mr. Randall said I could do this. If you have a problem with it, you should take it up with him." As we've probably learned by now, I have no issue with pawning my problems off on other people.

"Oh, I will," she said.

Once that was done I closed and locked the door again, then returned to my cast. I didn't give Sam the chance to tell me how much Hope was going to make me regret that. "Seeing how I'm new to this whole directing thing," I said, "Mr. Randall and Ms. Monroe have agreed to let us work on the stage most of next week." I didn't have to point out what a coup that was for us. Anne's classroom was a nice space, but it couldn't compare to being on the actual stage.

"That being the case," I continued, "today I want to work on the smaller moments, personal motivations and such. Things we *all* need to work on." I added the last bit for Belinda's benefit so she didn't think this was about her. Because it wasn't. True, it was more about her than it was about Sam and Jason. But it was actually more about me than anyone. I'd been so worried about everyone else's *opinion* of what I was doing that I wasn't paying enough attention to *what* I was doing.

"Let's start with Belinda's first entrance," I said. "We need to establish the triangle from the first moment all three of you are onstage together."

I walked them through the new blocking for the opening, staging the scene so they were in a subtle triangle. Seeing my image live and in person made me question it immediately. They were in too literal a triangle for no reason, which I pointed out.

"Why don't we try this," Jason suggested, moving himself over to where the bar would be to pour a drink. It wasn't a major move, but it opened up the scene and made Sam and Belinda's positions much more natural.

"That's it!" I said. "Do that. And let's take it from Belinda's entrance line."

We worked through the scene, integrating it into the existing blocking. Sam and Jason gave me plenty of suggestions for ways to make it better. We tried different movements and different placement. When we settled on something, I had Gary note it in the prompt book. I was watching the play get better and better right before my eyes. Even Belinda got into the swing of things, making her own suggestions and throwing in new ideas for Jason and Sam when she wasn't even onstage.

This was how I always imagined my rehearsals. It wasn't all perfect. Some problems had no easy solution. Some things didn't work as well as I hoped they would. But we were working. Without interruptions. Without all the second-guessing. I was beginning to think this thing was going to come together in time for opening night.

We were doing so well that I became immersed in the play. The outside world ceased to exist until Gary's wrist slid in front of my face. "Nice watch," I whispered.

"Thanks," he replied. "That's not what I'm showing you."

We were already a half hour over. "Yikes!"

The last thing any actor wants to hear is their director say "Yikes!" during a scene. Everyone froze and looked at me.

"Sorry!" I said. "It's not you. I didn't realize how much we'd run over." I checked my own watch to confirm the time. "We covered a lot today. Made some real progress."

"I can stay longer," Sam offered. "If you want to work some more."

"We still need to figure out that big kiss at the end," Jason said. I'm sure he was just being a good actor, but there was something somewhat *eager* in the way he said that. At least, that's how it sounded to me.

"Mr. Randall can't lock up until we're done," I said. All the other students and faculty were gone. I was pretty sure that the headmaster skipped out before last bell rang.

"We should work that first thing tomorrow," Sam said. Again, I wondered if the eagerness was in my imagination. "It's an important moment."

"Actually, I want to do something else tomorrow," I said. "I'd like to schedule a half hour with each of you to have one-on-one discussions about your characters. Talk about motivation. Answer any questions you might have. Generally make sure we're all on the same page when we get back into the auditorium Monday."

Everyone liked that idea. While they were scheduling time with Gary for the next day, Sam came over to me. "If you give me a ride home tomorrow, I can stay later so Jason and I can rehearse the kiss after you get done with the talks."

"It can wait till Monday," I said. "Ms. Monroe has the stage tomorrow so we wouldn't be able to work it properly. It's such an intimate moment, I'm afraid if we rehearse it here, it won't come through onstage." I was proud of myself for that one. It was part of the reason why I didn't want to rehearse the kiss. But it wasn't the whole reason.

"Are you sure?" she asked. Her skepticism radar was scanning the area.

"Jason's getting over a cold," I said. "I don't want you to catch it."

This was one excuse too many and Sam's skepticometer put her on full alert. "He got over that last week," she said, then added in a whisper so soft I had to strain to hear it. "Is this because of what Eric said last night? Because if you're worried about—"

I cut her off. "Sam, when have I ever worried about upsetting Eric's feelings? Seriously. This has nothing to do with him. I don't want you all getting used to actions that are probably going to have to change once we get onstage. That's all."

What can I say? Sam bought it. It probably helped that I'd spent most of her relationship hating her boyfriend. But now that I'd finally accepted them as a couple, I could see how much he made her happy and how well they worked together. Besides, I kind of liked having Eric around lately, and not because it was the only way to keep Drew hanging out too.

I'm not *that* selfish.

Perish the thought.

Artist Descending a Staircase
(Actually, It Was a Ladder)

"Hey, Bry, wait up!"

I tried ignoring the shout-out because the shouter was using a form of my name that I typically do not respond to. I tried for about .5 seconds before my curiosity got the best of me. It isn't often that Eric Whitman calls out to me in the halls between classes. Actually, it isn't *ever*. So you can see why I was intrigued.

"Yes?" I asked as I allowed him to catch up to me.

"You going to meet with Drew now?" he asked.

Great. Now that I wasn't letting him into rehearsals he was probably planning to crash private meetings about the show. Boy has some abandonment issues.

"That's the plan," I said, continuing toward the art room with haste.

"Hold up," he said, placing a hand on my arm. Not in the

same way Gary did two nights earlier. Just wanted to be clear about that. (As if there were any question.)

"I'm gonna be late," I said.

"He'll wait," Eric said as the hall started emptying in the direction of the pavilion for the senior/junior lunch shift. "I want to talk to you about the painting he's doing for the show."

"What about it?"

"It's kind of important."

For this I had to stop? *"I know.* I'm the director of the play. You've been to most of the rehearsals, you must have noticed that." Just because I was liking Eric more than I used to didn't mean I had to treat him any better.

"Not for the play," Eric said. "For him. He needs it for his portfolio. He hasn't really been working on his art—"

"For six years," I said, making it clear that I still knew a few things about my former best friend.

"Yeah, well, the colleges he's looking at want to see a whole bunch of stuff," Eric said, showing that he currently knew more about my former best friend than I did. "He needs more samples if he wants to impress the admissions boards. It's kind of bumming him out lately, if you haven't noticed."

Here I was thinking his mood had something to do with me.

Whoops.

"So what do you want me to do?" I asked. I mean, it was good information to know and all, but I was already going to meet with Drew to talk about the painting. There wasn't much more I could do with this news than feel like even more of an ass because I'd put it off.

"I wanted you to know that there's more riding on this than the play," he said, showing more depth than I tend to give him credit for and making me come over to his side even more. The guy is way too perfect to be true sometimes. "This is important to Drew. And if you still care—"

"*Don't* finish that sentence," I said with an intensity that scared us both. If he was going to call into question the level of *my* largely unreturned feelings of friendship toward Drew, all that goodwill I'd been extending him lately was going to be in serious jeopardy.

"He told you all this?" I said.

Eric looked at me like I'd gone insane. "Course not. We don't talk about that kind of stuff."

"Then why are you telling it to me?"

"Because. You. Do."

"Ah," I said. I couldn't argue that point.

"So, how did rehearsal go yesterday?" Eric asked, moving us to another topic that should not be discussed. "You know, since I'm no longer welcome."

I chose to ignore the dig. "Pretty good, actually. We got to work some of the moments that we hadn't really focused on yet."

"Like the ending?" he asked, deftly maneuvering the conversation to its real purpose.

What can I say? I threw him a bone. "We're saving that till we rehearse onstage next week. The kiss has to be faked so that it plays bigger than a real one. I'll probably have Jason block Sam from the audience so imaginations can make it more intense than it really is. Their lips won't even have to touch." That last part was a lie, but Eric was buying it. So long as he didn't add any more conflict to my already trauma-filled rehearsals, life would be good. And if it made him feel better in the process, well, that was an unexpected consequence I could put up with.

"Any chance I can swing by next week?" Eric asked, trying to be nonchalant.

"Do you like it when Sam watches you at soccer practice?" I asked.

"Yeah!" he said.

"And it doesn't distract you in the least?"

"Not one bit."

I waited.

"Maybe a little."

I waited some more.

"Okay. Fine."

"You're welcome to come opening night," I said. "And closing night."

"They're the same night," he reminded me. I didn't bother pointing out that this was an old joke around the theater, what with the One-Act Festival being a one night affair.

And on that note . . . . "If you'll excuse me," I said with a flourish of my hand. "Drew awaits."

"Can't you Drama Geeks just say 'See you later'?"

"Where's the style in that?" I asked with an exaggerated eye roll. It worried me that Eric laughed along with me. It was probably the first time in years that he and I had laughed together about anything. Now I was *really* worried that we were becoming friends.

The art room was empty when I got there, which I found somewhat annoying. Either Drew was later than I was, or he couldn't be bothered to wait for me and left. Not that it was my fault I was late. *His* best friend had been the one taking up my time.

Before I could work up a nice head of steam about Drew being inconsiderate, I heard a noise from the studio off the classroom. Maybe he'd already gotten to work, which would make me look like more of an ass for not thinking of that as one of the reasons for him not waiting in the classroom.

I made my way past the rows of empty tables to the art studio beyond.

Yes, our school has a fully stocked and professionally designed art studio, with skylights to provide natural lighting, a concrete floor with a drain for easy cleanup, and walls covered with shelving full of any material an artist could need. We *so* don't believe in the old saying that you have to suffer to create art. Unless by "suffer" you mean the pure misery of having to choose between a hundred different shades of red paint. Although, for the indecisive artist, all this excess could be hell.

"Drew?" I called out as I came into the empty studio. I was starting to work up that anger again since he was nowhere to be seen.

Then I heard a voice from above.

"Hey!"

There was a ladder to my right and a pair of familiar sneakers slightly above my eye level. I looked past those sneakers and up the attached leg to find the rest of Drew's skinny though toned body. He was searching through items on the tippy-top shelf of the wall unit.

"Hey," I replied, waiting for him to comment about my lateness.

I guess he was waiting for me to *apologize* for my lateness, because there was a significant silence that followed our greeting.

"What are you doing up there?" I asked the Nike Swoosh in my eye line.

"Scouting locations for an aerial assault," Drew replied. Ah, sarcasm. That was actually a good sign. Drew and I hadn't had a good banter in a while.

"If you drop a tub of paint on my head, I'm knocking you off that ladder," I warned him.

"You and what army?"

Okay. It wasn't particularly original or creative banter, but I could work with it.

"Much as I like conversing with your stylin' Nikes," I said, "how 'bout you join me back on terra firma?"

At my request he descended from on high with a bottle of black paint in his hand. He stopped when he reached the ground and looked me right in the eyes, which was also odd when considering his behavior of late. "Before you say anything stupid," he said. Always a good opening line. Tends to put one right on the defensive, you know? "I wanted to . . . well . . . thanks for letting me do this. It means a lot."

So much for defensive. It's not like I could work up any anger over that. It was also not like I had any say in the matter in the first place.

Still . . .

"I didn't do anything," I said. "Really. But I'm glad you're doing it. Seems fitting. Hope's play. I'm directing. Sam's in it."

"Now we just need to find a way to squeeze Eric in and the circle is complete."

"Yeah," I said. "Maybe we'll leave that particular circle incomplete. You've heard about this kiss at the end of the play, right?"

"Every. Day."

So it was as bad as I thought.

"Freaking out, huh?"

"The guy goes away all summer long and doesn't worry about her once," Drew said. "First play she's in since they became a couple and he gets all jealous."

"Although," I said, "it is kind of nice to see Mr. Perfect be insecure for once in his life."

The sheepish grin that broke out on Drew's face assured me that he felt the same.

"So you're applying to art school," I said.

The grin was gone. "Where'd you hear that?"

From you. The other night. And then Eric just confirmed it. "I didn't realize—"

"No," Drew said, leaning on the ladder. "It's okay. I'm

applying to art school, but I'm not really applying to art school."

Yeah. He lost me there too. "Try that again?"

"I'm applying to a lot of schools," he admitted, picking at some dry paint on the ladder.

"Waiting to see what sticks?"

"Trying to figure out what I want to do with my life."

I nodded. "Tell me about it."

His fingernails dug into the wood rung as he continued to work on the paint. "Like you don't know exactly what you're going to school for. It was all anybody could talk about back at the start of school this year." *Really?* Where was I? "You're going to be a director. Sam's going to be an actress. Hope a writer. Eric a soccer star."

"Yeah, but once he gets out of college, what's he going to do?" I asked. "Move to Europe where people actually watch the sport?"

"Maybe," Drew said. Man, that paint was totally stuck on the wood. "And if he doesn't, he's got his dad's business to fall back on."

I suspected a joke about a Fortune 500 company being a lame fallback option would not have been appreciated. "So you don't know what you want to be when you grow up," I said. "Is that why you've been all mopey-pants for the past month? So what? You and half the other seniors across the country."

"But not at this school," he said. "Name me one person at Orion who doesn't have their future mapped out right down

Paul Ruditis

to gross annual income. Do you get how much it sucks not to
know who you are? Who you want to be?"

"Just because the rest of us know what jobs we want doesn't
mean we have a clue about who we are," I said. Sometimes I
envied Eric and his friendship with Drew. I doubt they ever got
this philosophical.

"Like you have to worry about that," he said.

"What's that supposed to mean?"

"Never mind," he said, giving up on the ladder. He walked
over to a blank canvas resting on an easel. "This painting. Do
you know what you want?"

I wasn't ready to change the subject, but I wasn't going to
force Drew to talk about it if he didn't want to. We had plenty
of time to get to that. I did my best to put it out of my mind.

When the day had started, I'd known exactly what I wanted.
I could have described the painting in minute detail, right down
to the brush strokes. It truly was going to be an integral image
in the play and I'd spent a lot of time thinking about it. Which
is what happens when you spend no time talking about it with
the artist.

But that was *before* I ran into Eric in the hall. Before I realized that Drew was having this whole existential dilemma.
Now that it was time for me to put my thoughts into words,
the only thing going through my mind was how important
this piece was going to be for Drew's portfolio.

"I'll be fine with whatever you do," I said.

The director who fails to provide direction.

The Three Sisters

"These are private meetings," I said as Belinda entered Anne's classroom with her twin shadow, Alexis, not far behind.

"I'm here to talk hair," Alexis said.

"The production meeting is next Wednesday," I reminded her.

"But I'm seeing my stylist this weekend," she said. "It's Alfonse at José Eber and you know how hard it is to get time with him." I do? "I want to go over my ideas with him while I have the chance. You know, get an expert's take on things. Because it's *Alfonse*."

Notice how she had to name him twice in case I missed it the first time. Like I had a clue who *Alfonse* was. Probably some guy whose real name was Alfred. Oh, and she punctuated that last *Alfonse* by getting comfortable in the seat I'd set out for Belinda.

I couldn't imagine any conversation she and I would have

about hair being long enough that she'd need to sit down for it. To let her know we'd be keeping it brief, I remained standing. Poor Belinda was savvy enough to take in the situation and not know what to do. She wound up leaning on Anne's desk, even though she was the twin who should have sat.

"Let's start with Sam, since she needs the most work," Alexis said.

"Sam's doing her own hair," I said, having already discussed this with her earlier in the week.

"I'm the hair designer," she reminded me.

"Yes, you are," I said without commenting on how annoyed I was about that. Okay, maybe she could detect it in my tone. A little. "But Sam puts a lot of work into her characters. And part of that is designing the look."

"So you're saying Belle doesn't take this as seriously as Sam?" Alexis asked, teeth bared. Belinda covered her face in embarrassment.

"I didn't say that at all." I did direct that comment more to Belinda than Alexis though.

Alexis wasn't buying it. "You know, you—"

"Don't," Belinda pled.

Alexis glared at her sister now. I wasn't sure if Alexis genuinely cared about Belinda or if she just liked to pick fights. I was leaning toward the fights. "Fine," Alexis said. "We'll move on to that mop of hair that Jason wears."

"He's not cutting it," I said defensively. I didn't know if Jason would be willing to trim his hair or not. He takes his acting seriously enough that he'd shave his head for a role, so

I was pretty sure he wouldn't mind. But we were in a power struggle. Besides, I couldn't imagine the artist that he was playing would spend too much time on his hair.

"I'd like to hear him tell me that," she replied. "I was thinking a nice faux-hawk. But with style. Maybe bleach the tips."

"I'll leave that to him," I said to save myself from the argument. She was cutting into my meeting time with Belinda and I was hoping to get things moving along.

"Now, for Belinda," Alexis said as she got up and came around to play with her sister's hair. Alexis rambled on for a good five minutes, tugging Belinda's head this way and that. It gave me great insight into what their childhood slumber parties must have been like for poor Belinda, but I didn't have a clue what Alexis was talking about in the long run. Granted, the look of the characters is important to the play, but once she started braiding Belinda's hair in front of me, I kind of lost focus. Whatever small amount of my attention she still had five minutes into her diatribe was totally gone when I saw Hope come up to the door.

"I thought this was another closed rehearsal," Hope said, throwing the first punch in Round 592 of the Rivera/Connors Twins Championship Brawl. Which left me wondering how I wound up in the middle of the ring.

"Alexis is just here to talk about hair and then *she's leaving*," I said to both of them.

"Well, then, let's talk hair," Hope said to Alexis. "Your roots are showing."

Okay, even I had to admit that was a weak punch. Alexis

has been naturally blond since birth. I expected more from Hope. What I didn't expect was the reaction from Alexis. She recoiled as if Hope had just turned it into a knife fight. "Take that back!" she shrieked. "You *know* my hair is one hundred percent natural, you Goth freak!"

Goth-Ick, *actually*, I thought.

Seeing how I wasn't needed for this, I leaned beside Belinda on Anne's desk and we took in the show. The insults flew back and forth for another few zings until, I guess, the noise had carried to Ms. Monroe's classroom down the hall.

"What is going on in here?" she asked, blowing into the room with her bitty baby bump in the lead. "Bryan, weren't you supposed to be having private meetings this afternoon, to discuss character?"

I immediately straightened up. "That was the plan."

"Then why are Hope and Alexis here?" she asked me, like I had a clue. Then again, as director, I guess it had been kind of my role to play mediator instead of captive audience.

Hope started to supply an answer: "We were—"

"This is very disrespectful to your director," she said to both Hope and Alexis. "Very disrespectful. And to your sister who is supposed to be using this time to work on her character. You're both being very selfish." Hope didn't correct her by throwing "step" in front of "sister." It wasn't like Ms. Monroe to speak with such fury in her voice. She tended to shy away from the students and the power their parents held because she needed the job. I'd be tempted to blame it on hormones, but that would be rather sexist of me. I'll let you draw your own conclusions on that one. Especially when she said with pure venom, "You both should leave the building. Now."

Hope, knowing better, left the room without a word. Alexis on the other hand . . .

"But I'm her ride," she said, indicating her sister.

"I'm sure Bryan would be happy to take her home," she said. "Or Gary. Where is Gary?"

"I told him I wouldn't need him for the meetings," I said, then turned to Belinda. "It's okay. I can take you. If you don't mind waiting while I talk to Jason and Sam."

"I can catch a ride with Holly when she's done with rehearsal," Belinda said, once again trying not to make waves. "You should go, Alexis. Before Hope takes the car."

"Crap!" Alexis bolted from the room. If I know Hope—and I do—she was already long gone.

"Thank you," I said to Ms. Monroe once the dust had settled.

She indicated that she wanted me to join her out in the hall. So I did. "I understand that dealing with some of these personalities can be . . ."

"A nightmare?"

"I was going to say 'a challenge,'" she replied. "But if you want to pursue directing professionally, then you're going to have to learn how to deal with it. Think of this as a trial by fire."

"Yeah, but I'm the one they keep firing at," I said.

"You'll do fine," she said, giving me a bop on the fedora before she went back to her rehearsal. When I returned to the classroom, Belinda was already seated at a desk with her script out in front of her and a pencil in hand.

She looked up at me with sad eyes. "I'm—"

I held up a hand. "Don't say it. You have as much control over Alexis as I have over Hope. There's nothing to apologize for." As I took the desk I'd set up opposite hers, I realized that wasn't entirely true. "Scratch that. I do have to apologize. For the other night. What I was saying to Gary—"

"It's okay," she said quickly.

"No. You and me . . . we don't have these moments to, like, talk. Ever. Let's try to get through it without polite-ing each other to death. I want to make it clear. If I didn't think you could do this, I would never have cast you. Ever."

"What? You don't enjoy risking your life with Hope?"

"Not usually," I said. "You're good. You're real good. What you heard . . . I was saying that you didn't have the same experience as Sam and Jason. Give it time. You might even be some competition in the future."

"We have a week and a half," she replied.

"Oh, not for this play," I said lightly. "I'm not that talented a director to make you that good in so little time. But keep working on it and by the spring show you might even give Sam a reason to worry. Well, maybe not Sam, but Holly will definitely be gunning for you."

"Just promise me you'll take me in when Holly excommunicates me from her inner circle."

I put a hand to my heart. "I swear. Besides, we *have* to take you in. It's in the Drama Geek code. We accept all rejects."

"Good to know," Belinda said.

And then we laughed.

That's right, I said *laughed*. I was sharing a laugh with Belinda Connors. We weren't in hysterics or anything, just a mild tittering, really. But it was an unusual experience for the two of us. First laughing with Eric and now with Belinda. Someone must have been pumping nitrous oxide through the school ventilation system.

I was actually enjoying myself so much that I stopped thinking. "Can I ask you a question?"

And she stopped laughing. "Yes?" she said with all the tentativeness that that question mark implies.

"What is the deal with you two and Hope?" I asked. "I wasn't all that close to Hope back when you and Alexis moved in, and she's never been particularly open with the backstory."

Belinda paused to think about her answer.

No. That's not the right way to describe what I saw going on in her eyes. She already knew the answer. She was deciding whether to share it with me.

I guess she thought I could be trusted, because she didn't hold back. "Because Alexis is a bitch," Belinda said. I about fell out of my chair. Belinda didn't use words like that. She didn't often partake in the name-calling. She left that to Holly and her sister. And I knew that she in particular hated the "B" word. So, consider me even more shocked when she used it again. "She's always been a bitch. A spoiled brat. Everything had to be her way. When my mom and Hope's dad met, I couldn't wait to have another sister. Maybe then I'd get a say in things. You know, two against one and all."

Somehow, I couldn't see her and Hope teaming up on anything.

"But Hope was mad from the start that we were moving in," she continued. "She thought we were taking over her space, which we kind of were. I once heard her dad tell my mom that we all should have moved into a new house instead of us moving into theirs. But that was months after we were already there." I'd heard enough about this time period from Hope to know the damage was already done by then.

"Hope was full on *Hope* the day we moved in," Belinda said. "Alexis immediately went after her by stealing her diary and broadcasting everything Hope had written about us to our mom. It wasn't very nice."

"Probably didn't help that the moving truck had run over her dog," I said, revealing what little I did know about that time.

"No, that didn't help at all." She was laughing again when she said that, but it wasn't a cruel laugh. She wasn't reveling in the death of a dog. It was more a laugh of frustration. Like she regretted how she had no real blame in the situation that, after years and years, had spiraled out of control. "So it was Hope against us from day one. If anything, it made me and Alexis closer. For what that's worth."

"Funny," I said, though it wasn't, "I never thought there was a time when you actually would have *wanted* to be Hope's sister."

"I still do," she said. "You think I like all the yelling and the hate? It's not a nice way to live."

"No," I said. "I'm sure it's not."

As much as I wanted to continue bonding, a glance at the clock told me we were going to run over on time if we didn't start soon. And the play was the reason we'd gathered in the first place. At the very least, I wanted to work on Belinda's chicken-necking problem. "Belinda," I said, "we'd better get to work."

"You can call me Belle, you know."

"Belle?"

"Everybody does."

"*Everybody?*" I asked. I mean, sure, I'd heard people call her that before, but *every*body?

"I kind of hate going by Belinda."

Which is probably why we always called her that, come to think of it. Funny how, in my mind, whenever anyone called her Belle, I heard Belinda.

"Why didn't you say anything?" I asked. "If you would have told us—"

"No one ever told me to call Samantha, Sam," she said. "I just heard other people do it and started doing it myself."

Touché.

School for Scandal

Those planets must have kept aligning in strange and wondrous ways because Monday started out weird and just got weirder. And most of it happened before I set foot inside school. Seriously. It could have been a word problem:

The distance from the student parking lot to the main entrance is approximately the length of one half of one city block. In the time that it takes Bryan Stark to get from point A (Electra) to point B (the main entrance), how much drama can he encounter?

Answer: A whole heck of a lot.

It all began the moment I stepped out of point A: Electra.

In a coincidence of horrible timing, Hope pulled up beside me in the pink and purple marshmallow on wheels that Alexis had picked out as the Rivera/Connors girls' car. Hope's dad could more than afford a vehicle for each child, but it clearly was a lesson on sisterhood in the form of a tricked-out Mini Cooper. (And yes, it was a cruel trick indeed.) As the Rivera/Connors girls stepped out of the car, three things of note happened. One for each girl, I guess.

1. Belinda . . . I mean, *Belle*, gave me a warm good-morning hug hello, causing . . .
2. Hope to growl (yes, you read that right) at me. Which is why I almost missed . . .
3. Alexis stepping out of the car with her blond hair shredded.

Odd angles and razor-sharp cuts may be all the rage in some sectors, but this was taken to an extreme, even for L.A. Alexis's head kind of resembled that origami flower that Sam had made for me the other day. It was all I could do not to bust out laughing in her face.

"And how is *Alfonse* these days?" I asked, referencing the stylist to the stars she'd been so thrilled that she was visiting before the visit.

"Shut it," she replied as she pushed past me.

Belle must have recognized the horror in my eyes, because she quickly said, "I'll be doing my own hair on show night."

"Oh, thank God."

As Hope and Belle split off in different directions, I turned toward school and came face-to-face with Drew.

"Good morning!" he said in a way too cheery voice for first thing in the day. Certainly more cheery than he'd been in the past month.

"Morning," I groaned, which was the acceptable greeting for any time prenoon.

"Cancel your lunch plans," he said. "I have something to show you in the art room."

"I was planning on lunch with you guys in the pavilion like always," I pointed out. "I can shift a few things." Then he gave me a rather hard pat on the back and hurried off more alive than I'd seen him in a while. He looked good. And happy.

And good.

My popularity continued to grow as Gary sidled up to me and latched on to my arm, until he realized he was latching on to my arm in the middle of a crowded parking lot, and let go. "One more week," he said. "Don't forget."

"Like I could forget when the show goes up," I said.

"Who's talking about the show? I meant the cast party. When you are no longer my boss and officially fair game."

These people were way too perky for a Monday morning. "What's with you?"

"Just happy to see you!" he said. "I'm going to ask Mrs. Brown to let me out a few minutes before last bell so I can have the stage set for rehearsal to begin as soon as everyone's there. Hey, there's Madison. Gotta go." He gave my shoulder a squeeze and ran off to meet his friend as I went up the concrete staircase.

Already, I'd been hugged, slapped, and squeezed, and I still hadn't made it to point B: the main entrance.

The morning perkiness took a noticeable turn when I saw my two leads huddled together off to the side of the front doors. Point B was so close. All I had to do was continue walking on the path I was on. A straight line. That's all it would take. They were probably just going over the script. But it wouldn't hurt to see if they needed any help.

Should I have been worried that they broke apart the moment they saw me?

"Hey!" I said, trying not to be suspicious. "What's up?"

"Nothing," they said in wonderfully horrific unison.

"I got to get to class," Jason said, even though we were all on the same timetable. He left before I could say anything else.

"What was that about?" I asked Sam.

"Later," she said. Finally, someone who was appropriately curt and surly for the time of day. I would have pressed further, but I felt another presence behind me. Any guesses who it might be? It shouldn't be hard. We're almost out of characters.

"Hey, you!" Eric said, brushing past me and giving Sam a Monday morning kiss that suggested they hadn't seen much of each other over the weekend. Considering I hadn't done anything with her outside of work Saturday, it made me awful curious about how she'd occupied the rest of the weekend.

"See you," Sam said as she and Eric went off to school just as Suze came up beside me with some cloth swatches of what I assumed were going to become costumes. "Just the guy I wanted to see," she said.

I was just basking in the Monday morning love.

But as Sam gave me a glance back over her shoulder, I wondered if I was the only one.

Suze and I entered point B together, with me wondering what new fun the day had in store.

The rest of the morning continued to play out in the same bizarre manner. Random smiles in the hall from Gary and Drew counterbalanced by snarls from Hope and Alexis. Belle said hi so many times that even Holly looked confused. But mostly I was noticing the way that Jason and Sam were pointedly avoiding each other. And if I was noticing, I suspected that other people were noticing as well.

When I saw Sam walking, unaccompanied, to drama I hurried to catch up with her. Before I could get a word out, we came to an intersection that Eric and Jason were also approaching from opposite directions. I guess Jason didn't see Eric, because he decided to stop avoiding and went straight for Sam at the same time her boyfriend came into the scene. We all nearly collided as a result. Suddenly life had become a farce.

Well, maybe it wasn't all that sudden.

"Hi!" Sam said, greeting everyone at once.

Seeing the distress evident on her face, I swooped in. "Jason!" I said. "I was hoping I'd run into you. Walk with me to drama. I want to talk about the play." Yeah, that was wonderfully vague. By the time we pulled away from the happy couple, I'd managed to come up with an excellent excuse.

"You've seen Alexis this morning?" I asked.

"Who hasn't?" he replied, gentlemanly enough not to laugh about her new do.

"I wanted to make sure you understood that you don't have to let her touch your hair," I said. "In case you were worried."

He nodded. "I wasn't. But it's good to know for sure. I was thinking of wearing it . . ." Seeing how a conversation about hair isn't all that interesting, let's sum it up by saying that Jason takes his characters very seriously and had a lot of suggestions for the overall look, which more than covered our walk to class and even the first few minutes while we waited for everyone else to arrive and settle down.

Sam was one of the last people into class. Even though we'd been sitting together in drama since almost day one, she saw me with Jason and took a seat on the opposite side of the room. By Hope. The other person I'd usually be sitting right beside in that class.

I was more than accustomed to aggressive Hope. But this new passive side to her personality was somewhat disturbing.

Class was not nearly as eventful as what went on in the school halls. As soon as Mr. Randall released us for lunch, I grabbed Sam by the arm and pulled her, somewhat unwillingly, to her mom's classroom. I moved so quickly that the last few stragglers from Anne's class were still packing up when we arrived.

"This is a surprise," Anne said, welcoming us into her room. "Did you two come to join me for lunch?"

"Actually, Bryan was hoping you could let us have your room for a few minutes."

Anne took in the situation, seeing that my hand was still firmly clasped to her daughter's arm. "Only a *few* minutes?"

"Yes," Sam said definitively.

"I can eat in the teachers' lounge," Anne said, grabbing a bag from her closet. "You two take all the time you need."

"Thanks!" I said brightly so I didn't scare Anne any more than I probably already had. The last thing Sam would want was to have her mom quizzing her later about our behavior, but I was dying to know what was going on.

"What did you do?" I asked, trying not to come across too intensely.

I failed.

"Don't be mad," Sam said.

Another one of those phrases that's never good to open a conversation with.

"Jason and I got together at his place to rehearse on Sunday," she said as if it were the end of the world or something.

I let out a breath of relief. "Is that all? Don't worry. I'm not offended. I want you guys to work on your characters. It's okay if I'm not there, as long as you don't change anything too much or fight me when I don't like what you come back with. Maybe you should work with Belle some time. It might give her more confidence."

"Belle?"

"Belinda."

"When did you . . . never mind. That's not all." She took a breath. "We worked the part we hadn't gotten to in rehearsal yet."

It wasn't difficult for me to figure out which part she was talking about. "You kissed Jason?" This was not good.

"I *rehearsed* with Jason," she said.

"You rehearsed the kiss!" I insisted.

"It was going so well," she said. "When we got to the end, we just kept going. We were in the moment. It made sense to work the scene through."

Oh, it made *total* sense. The kiss that I had been trying so hard to avoid them doing in a controlled atmosphere . . . on a huge stage . . . in front of a small audience of people . . . with a director telling them the best way to fake it. They had gone and done it themselves, in a small room with no one around.

I needed to sit down. So I did. On Anne's desk.

"You're mad," she said.

But I wasn't. "No," I said. "But . . . you kissed Jason."

"It was just a rehearsal," her mouth insisted, but the rest of her . . .

"You wouldn't be making this big a deal out of it if it was just a rehearsal," I said. "If it was just a rehearsal you would have called me yesterday. Then you would have told me to get over it and moved on. If it was just a rehearsal, you wouldn't look so guilty right now. And don't tell me it's because you feel like you betrayed me as your director by rehearsing behind my back. That is way too lame an excuse."

Sam sat beside me on the desk. "Why can't I ever manage to keep anything from you?"

"Beats me," I said. "But sometimes I wish you would."

There were so many things going on in my mind. Questions. Consolations. And yet, the one thing that kept running around up there was why she had to wait until I actually started to become—I can't believe I'm going to say this—*friends* with Eric to go and betray him.

Damn her!

"What am I going to do?" she asked.

"A kiss is just a kiss," I said.

"Do you have to make a joke out of everything?"

I didn't think answering yes would have been appropriate. "Seriously. It was a kiss. You never said you had feelings for Jason before. A kiss isn't going to change that."

She hopped off the desk. "You don't understand."

"What don't I understand?" I said, hopping down too. "You kissed him. It was intense. It's an intense moment in the play. You don't have to walk around feeling all guilty about it. Maybe it meant nothing to Jason."

"It meant something to Jason."

"Oh, God," I said. "You didn't—"

"No! We only kissed. One time. Then we both got uncomfortable, so I left. That's it."

It was enough.

"But you've *never* talked about Jason like that before," I insisted.

"You keep going back to that," she said.

"You've known him for more than two years," I reminded her.

"He was with Wren most of that time," she said.

"Like you've never told me about a guy you were crushing on who had a girlfriend," I said. "Not buying it. Feelings like this don't come out of nowhere." Because if they did, I wouldn't be having such a difficult time convincing myself to give Gary a try. "You were just in character. You both are pretty intense about acting. You were probably confused by the kiss and thought it meant something else."

"You wouldn't say that if you'd ever been kissed."

The banging I believed to be in my head was actually coming from the door. Feeling like we both needed a break, I went to get it.

"What are you doing?" Drew asked as I opened the door. I quickly checked behind him to make sure his shadow wasn't lurking. The last thing we needed was Eric on the scene . . . making a scene.

"How did you know we were here?" I asked. "You didn't hear us through the door?" The ramifications of that would be deadly. Okay, slight exaggeration, but it would be *baaaaaad*.

"I ran into Sam's mom and asked if she knew where you were," Drew said. "Are you coming?"

"Coming where?" I asked.

I never witnessed someone deflate in front of me, but he sure looked deflated . . . in the metaphorical sense.

"To see the painting," he said.

Which is why he wanted me to meet him in the art room at lunch.

"You finished? Already?"

"Spent the whole weekend working on it," he said proudly.

"It's okay," Sam said. "You can go." Her words said "go," but her tone said "please don't leave me right now because I don't know what to do and how I'm going to get through this and I could really use a friend right now to lean on and possibly cry on his shoulder a bit as well."

Or maybe I could have been reading a bit more into the tone than was actually there. But still, she clearly needed me to stay. And I needed to stay. We had some unfinished business.

Of course, staying with her meant abandoning Drew. Knowing how much this painting meant to him, it was something I couldn't do.

But I did.

"Can I swing by after school?" I asked.

Whatever air was left in him deflated even more.

"I was kind of hoping—"

"I know," I said softly with a glance back at Sam. "But you know I wouldn't blow off your artwork for no reason. This is important."

Drew nodded. We may have had our problems over the years, but history had proven that we were there for each other when we needed to be. "But you have rehearsal after school," he reminded me.

"I can be late," I said. "I'm tight with the director."

Drew gave me a smile that told me he was fine, then left with a good-bye nod to Sam.

"Now, where were we?" I asked as I shut the door. "Oh, right. I can't help you because I've never had a real kiss."

"That's not—"

"No, I get it," I said. "What are the qualifications I need to possess in order to make you feel better? Do I have to have a boyfriend? Do I have to be a girl?"

"Well, the first qualification is that you have to be nicer to me," she said.

Okay, maybe I was being a little touchy, but it was a touchy subject. Granted, I never told her the whole truth about my kissing history, but she didn't have to throw her suspicions in my face. Even if they weren't entirely accurate.

"What are we going to do about this?" I asked. And I was being nicer.

"It's not really a 'we' problem," she said.

"You think I'm going to keep directing you to kiss Jason for the rest of the week?" I asked. "And do you think it's not going to be noticeable if I keep skipping a run-through of the climactic end to the play? It's a 'we' problem whether you like it or not. Eric's already jealous. And that was before he had something to be jealous about."

"He doesn't—"

"*Potentially* has something to be jealous about," I corrected. "Either way, you need to sort out your feelings. If you're not sure about Eric, you need to let him know. And if you like Jason, well . . ."

"*I need to know.*"

As You Like It

"I'm here!" I announced forcefully as if my excitement would make up for blowing Drew off at lunch.

"So I see," he said, matching my enthusiasm with his lack thereof. It was his way of letting me know he wasn't buying it. Either his shoes became newly interesting to him again, or he was upset that I'd missed our appointment.

Hey! I had a lunch appointment. That's one of those things that makes me a real live amateur, professional director. (If only I'd kept the appointment.)

"I'm ready to be dazzled," I said with my smile on high beam.

"Then you've come to the wrong place," Drew said, picking his head up from the direction of his shoes. "I am a serious artiste. I do not dazzle. I touch the emotional core through my artwork and move the viewer."

Yeah, right. "Dazzle me," I said.

He shook his head, giving up. "This way." Drew led me back to the studio, where he'd set up the painting. It was resting on the same easel it had been on the other day, but the canvas wasn't blank anymore. It was a work of art.

The painting was an amalgam of light and shadow. The edges were the deepest black that faded to gray as your eye moved to the middle. He didn't go for the obvious with triangles and jagged edges, like Alexis's hair. The shapes on the canvas were all rounded and curved, with gentle lines and swirls growing out of the center. The effect was three distinct pictures in the one piece that, at the same time, blended together and fractured apart, reflecting the compli- cated relationships in the play.

It was soft. And fragile. And moving.

And almost perfect.

"It's beautiful," I said.

"But?"

Wow. I'd packed all my enthusiasm into that one.

"Well," I said. "It could use some color."

"Achromatic," Drew said. "It means 'without color.' Which means black, white, and gray."

"I know what the word means," I said, even though I'd never heard it before I read Hope's work. "But the play is called *Achromantic*. To play up the romance aspect. So I think it would work better if we added some colors. Like some blue or green to go with the rest of the set."

"You did not just ask me to change my painting so it would match the couch. No. I refuse to believe that's what you want."

"But it's not just a painting," I insisted. "It is a set piece. It has to work within the context of the play."

"And you couldn't have told me this before I spent all weekend working on it?"

"Because I didn't know what you were going to do," I said. "I wanted you to have a chance to create something of your own. To impress those college admissions people. All I'm asking for is a little color. That's it."

"The piece is done," Drew said. "Finished. I can't go adding a splash of color on a whim. Would you have asked da Vinci to add a little more of a smile to the *Mona Lisa*?"

I'd gone and created a monster. "You did not just compare yourself to Leonardo da Vinci!"

"You know what I mean!"

Why were we screaming?

"Drew," I said, taking it down a notch. "This is a beautiful painting. It really is. But I want it to be perfect for the play. For Hope's play. You get that, right?"

Nothing.

"You'll make the change?"

Nada.

"Please?"

Finally he spoke: "As you wish."

Great. He was *Princess Bride*–ing me. We used to say that back when we were kids and one of us felt like the other was getting too bossy. It wasn't until we were older that we got the whole part about how in the movie when Wesley said that to Buttercup he was really saying "I love you." Once we realized that, Drew immediately stopped using it, though I may have slipped every now and then.

But Drew wasn't exactly using it now with love in his voice.

"Thank you," I said as I left him behind to make the change . . . and to stew in his anger.

But really, I was the director. Weren't we all supposed to be working toward *my* vision? Okay, I could have given him more direction earlier, but I honestly wanted him to have the freedom to create. All I was asking for was one minor tweak. A piddling change. Was that so wrong?

I tried to put it out of my mind as I hurried to Hall Hall for rehearsal. When I got there, I was glad to see Jason leading everyone through warm-up exercises onstage. I was even happier to find that even though I hadn't been there, Gary had made sure everyone took the "Closed Rehearsal" signs on the auditorium doors seriously, as nobody was there sticking their noses in our business.

Not wanting to disturb my cast—or join in the workout myself—I silently took a seat in the front row while they finished up. This gave me time to observe everyone.

I didn't like what I was seeing.

They were all going through the warm-ups well enough. For Sam and Gary (who'd joined in even though he didn't have to), everything was second nature. Belinda . . . I mean Belle, took a while to get up to speed on some of the voice and movement exercises. She'd only had limited experience with them, having learned a few during the Summer Theatrical Program. But a lot of the stuff Jason was doing hadn't been covered back then and she was a total newbie.

As nice as it was seeing them all work together as a team, there was a little too much teamwork going on for my comfort level. Sam and Jason kept doing that thing where one would look to see if the other was looking, then look away so the other didn't see that he or she was looking. Furtive glances all over the place. I'm pretty sure I was the only one who noticed, particularly since I was specifically keeping an eye out for that kind of thing.

At one point I thought Belle had caught them, because she was giving Jason a funny look. The last thing I needed was for Belinda to catch on. I trusted her now a lot more than I used to, but the more people who suspected that something was going on, the more potential there was for someone to slip and talk about it.

It was the second glance that changed my mind.

Belle liked Jason.

The triangle of Hope's play was playing itself out right in front of me onstage, but in real life. This I could do something with. If I could get Belle—I'm sorry, but she's *so* Belinda to me—together with Jason, that could be the way to keep Sam and Eric coupled. I know. Never thought I'd hear myself say those words either. But after months of fighting it I was finally ready to accept that Eric and Sam were pretty good together. Besides, the subtext of a real-life triangle working under the play would make it a performance to remember.

Not that I was planning to trade on my friends' genuine

emotional turmoil to make for a better production. That was just a lucky coincidence.

"Good job, everyone," Jason said, signaling that the warm-ups were over.

"Yes," I agreed. "Good job. Thanks, Jason, for running through the exercises. If you want to do that every day we're in here, that would be great."

"Consider it done," he said with a salute.

"Now we should get to work," I said.

Gary came off the stage to join me. "We left off the other day at the end of the play. Do you want to start there?"

I could see both Sam and Jason watching me intently, waiting for my response. "Not quite yet," I said. "I want to go back to the beginning and do a run-through with all the blocking we did last week. Is everyone okay with that?"

Not only were they okay but two of them were positively relieved.

We took it from the beginning with Belle's offstage opening line. Since we were back in the auditorium, I had Gary open the curtain on her to make sure she could get around it in time for her entrance. Good thing we did that because we ran into an unexpected problem. The curtain took slightly longer to open than we'd anticipated, which threw off the timing of the opening scene. We'd blocked out a certain number of objectives for Sam and Jason to hit in their flirtatious dance before Belle entered. To cover it we were either going to have to start the scene after the curtain opened, Belle was going to have to take longer pauses when she spoke, or . . .

"Oh, dear," I said aloud.

Again, not something a cast wants to hear their director say.

"What's wrong?" Gary asked.

I addressed my response to everyone. "I'm going to ask Hope if she can add a line or two to help with the staging." Yep. I was going to approach Hope about altering her script. Her locked script. The one that I'd told everyone we would not be changing.

Oy.

Once we got past that hiccup, we managed to run through the play rather quickly. All of my actors had taken our discussions from Friday to heart and made adjustments to their characters accordingly. Belle was by far the best. And I don't just mean because she'd finally gotten over the whole chicken-necking deal. Either I was seeing her differently now that we'd talked or she had made some dramatic change on her own this past weekend, but she was approaching Sam and Jason's acting level much more quickly than I'd thought she would. There were times I was so amazed by her, I lost track of the others in the scene altogether. (But don't tell my teacher about that. Or my actors.) When she finished her big monologue, even Gary had let out a little "Wow."

Not that everything was perfect. Some of the staging wasn't working in the larger space. Some of the dialogue was lost because I had the actors facing slightly upstage. Some of the movements disappeared in the bigger space. But if those were the only problems we had to fix, the play would easily be set in time for the festival.

Which is why I stopped them before it could all unravel.

"All right," I said as Belle exited the stage. "We're good for today."

"But what about the ending?" Gary asked. "We need to do the kiss."

I held up my finger in the internationally recognized sign for "Wait a second." I called up to the stage, "Belle, you're dismissed for the day. I want to work on a few things with Jason and Sam."

At this Belle looked confused, while Sam and Jason experienced more relief.

"You can go too," I told Gary in a softer tone. "This kiss is going to be awkward enough. I don't want them to have to do it for the first time in front of a bunch of people. Besides, I don't want Belle to think I'm just sending her away. You know?"

"Gotcha," he said. "A first kiss should be a more private thing. I know that's my plan for the first kiss I have with you."

Gulp.

I couldn't manage to actually piece together any words while Gary and Belle collected their things and went up the aisle to the back exit. Once I heard the door click behind them, I pushed Gary's exit line out of my mind and turned my attention to my remaining actors. Sam was about to say something, but I stopped her. "Let's wrap this up so we can go."

We went over their motivations up to that point as I walked halfway to the back of the auditorium. I wanted to make sure whatever we were doing was going to read at least that far. In theater, actions have to be larger than life so the people in the back row can see them, but not so large that the people in the front row laugh over how ridiculous it looks. I was afraid about how large this kiss was going to have to be and concerned about what I was going to encourage.

"You might want to underplay it to start," I called to them. "Ease into things."

"Wouldn't it be easier to start big and take it down?" Jason asked.

"Why don't we just show you what we came up with over the . . . " Sam trailed off, clearly not wanting to bring up the unspoken moment. "Before."

"Um . . ." I said. Then I heard a voice squeak behind me.

"Sorry," Belle said in her traditional way of apologizing for being alive. "I left my scarf. Don't let me stop you."

I never understood the fashion of wearing a scarf during the day when it wasn't that cold out. In my opinion, scarves should only be worn with a coat. But I didn't say anything about that to Belle because I didn't want to encourage her to stay any longer than necessary.

I also didn't want to have the kiss conversation in front of anyone, but I knew all the trust I'd built with her would come crashing down if I stopped talking while she was around. So I did continue talking, but I was mainly rambling on about the history of kissing on the stage, a subject I knew absolutely nothing about. I was so preoccupied by creating my fanciful story to fill the time that Belle was in the room that I barely noticed when she'd left.

I certainly wasn't aware that she didn't close the door all the way behind her.

I concluded my speech by warning them, "Don't worry about it feeling real to you on the stage, it has to *look* real to me out in the audience."

They both nodded in an exaggerated manner to let me know I'd made my point, then they went into the scene.

I was so nervous, I needed to stand as they approached the final moment. It was amazing watching them get right back into the play at the same emotional point that they had been building to earlier. I guess some people can turn it on and off like a switch, as the saying goes.

I clasped the chair in front of me as we approached the kiss. It was an important moment, but I doubt that I would have been tense if it weren't for all the drama that had been surrounding it.

I braced myself as they went in.

They didn't turn away from the audience. Sam didn't hide herself behind Jason's back. They went in full force, but tentatively. As if they were unsure of what the kiss meant for their characters . . . and for themselves. It took forever for their lips to touch, but when they did, I swear the ground beneath me jolted. There was so much passion on that stage.

My fears for the end of the play were immediately gone. The characters were feeling it onstage, and it was certainly coming across in the audience. The kiss went on maybe a bit longer than it should have, but it was only a matter of degrees.

When they finally broke apart, I burst out into furious applause that echoed through the empty space. There was nothing to tell them to change. Nothing to work. It was the perfect moment to end the play with.

"And . . . curtain!" I yelled over my clapping even though there was no one there to close them. It didn't matter. I was wrapped up in the moment. I was thrilled and I wanted them to know it.

My actors weren't basking in the applause the way they should have been. In fact they didn't seem to notice I was reacting at all. They were both focused on something behind me. I didn't have to turn to know what it was. The horror, coupled with guilt, on Sam's face told me everything I needed to know.

Eric had come into the auditorium behind me.

He had watched the whole thing.

Betrayal

"She left the door open on purpose," Hope insisted the next day. We'd gathered for lunch in Anne's classroom, forcing Sam's mom to retreat to the teachers' lounge for the second day in a row.

"I don't think Belle would do that," I said. "Alexis? Definitely. But Belle . . ."

"When the hell did you start calling her Belle?"

"That rhymes!" I said in a lame attempt to lighten the mood. I'd thought that Hope and I had called a truce to help Sam with her boyfriend troubles. But Hope was clearly having trouble getting past the fact that I'd banished her from rehearsals. Of course, it didn't help when I asked her this morning if she could slightly tweak the opening of the play. My ears were still ringing from that one.

"He can tell," Sam said, bringing us back to the subject of our luncheon conversation. "He can tell it wasn't just acting. I tried to talk to him after rehearsal but he wouldn't answer his phone. He shut me down every time I went up to him today."

"It's not your fault," Hope said with one last glare at me. "You're confused. I wrote some damn fine characters. And you always throw yourself way into a role anyway. Maybe you threw yourself a bit too hard this time. That's all. Nothing to lose Eric over."

"What was he doing hanging around Hall Hall all afternoon anyway?" I asked, trying to build up the dislike I used to feel all the time for Eric. It would be so much easier to make him the villain in all this.

"Mom had to run some errands after school. He offered to take me home," Sam said, making Eric all the more Mr. Perfect. Not to mention, it explained why my car services were suddenly needed after rehearsal. Forty-five minutes of traffic on the PCH listening to Sam leave message after message for him from my cell phone was not fun. Good thing I've got a good cellular contract.

"The important thing is we need to figure out how you feel about Jason," I said. "You could wind up losing Eric over nothing. So tell me. Does Jason make you all squishy inside?"

"Yes," she said. "He's radiated my innards to the point where I'm melting from the inside out. Like a microwave oven."

"Sarcasm is not going to help," I said, which is a tad hypocritical coming from me, I know.

Sam looked at me. "It's just—"

"Yeah, yeah, yeah," I said. "I've never been in love. I've

never been kissed. Got it." I tried not to be angry, but I was. A wee bit hurt as well. She was acting like because she was in a relationship she had some exclusive membership in a secret club. A club where my opinion no longer mattered. Part of it was my fault, for not being entirely honest with her, but that's not the point. Sam's got all these rules about things she can talk to me about and things that are, as they would say in *Cabaret*: verboten. But her rules change on a whim. *Her* whim.

Not that I was trying to turn her pitiful situation around so that it was all about me. But sometimes I wondered when things did get to be all about me. I'd upset Hope because I kept her out of the rehearsals for *her* play. I can't help Sam because I don't meet *her* requirements for advice giving. Even Drew'd been giving me glares because I dared to suggest a change to *his* painting.

The only person who seemed to be putting me first was Gary. Which was another reason why it made no sense that I couldn't force myself to have feelings for him. Well, it made sense in the grand scheme, but it was damn annoying.

"Where do you go when you drift off like that?" Hope asked me.

And here I thought all these mental sidebars went unnoticed.

I ignored her. "I'm not buying it," I said to Sam. "Hope's right. You don't have feelings for Jason, you have feelings for his character. And Hope is also right that she wrote some damn fine characters."

"Don't think sucking up to me is going to make me any happier about making changes to my script," Hope said.

What can I say? I tried. "Duly noted."

But Sam wasn't saying anything . . . which I took as my cue.

"Look, if you'd prefer to talk to Hope about this alone, you can tell me."

Sam hit me with pleading eyes but couldn't bring herself to say the words.

Part of me was hurt by this. But another part of me didn't much mind. That part of me saw this as an opportunity.

"I get it," I said, standing. "I'm not the one you need right now. It's okay." I tried not to overplay it, as acting isn't my strong suit. "I'll leave you two to talk."

And I did. Because with Sam busy talking to Hope, I could get to work on my plan to save her relationship with Eric.

But, first . . .

"Hey!" I said as I stepped into the hall and right into Drew's path.

"I was just coming to find you," he said. He was in a much better mood than he'd been in when I left him the day before.

"Let me guess," I said. "You've finally snapped and are coming to kill me."

"Not yet," he replied. "But any day now, I'm sure." He was bouncing on the balls of his feet. "Aren't you going to ask me what I'm excited about?"

"Do I want to know?"

This earned me a slap on the shoulder. "I finished the painting!"

Relief washed over me. He'd made the changes. Now all I had to do was hope that I liked them. "Great! I was heading for the pavilion, but I can make a detour."

"No!" he said so loudly that I worried a teacher was going to come out and ask us why we were in the hall between classes.

"You came by to tease me with the news?" I asked.

"I came by to ask if I can show it to you before rehearsal," he said. "Onstage. Under the stage lights?"

With all that enthusiasm, how could I say no?

"No."

"Bryan!"

"Okay," I said with a laugh. "You can show me after school. I can't wait."

"Neither can I!" he said as he hurried off.

See? It's times like that when I understand why I don't have feelings for my associate stage manager. Even at his most excited, Gary's enthusiasm never gets to me the way Drew's does.

Sigh.

Now, on with my plan . . .

When I got to the pavilion, I was surprised to see Jason— one of the most popular guys in the class—sitting alone off to the side of the room, making notes in his script. It really shouldn't have been a shock, knowing how seriously he takes his craft, but that level of commitment to anything is very rare around Orion Academy. I almost hated to disturb him.

Almost.

But first I needed to find my other star. It wasn't difficult. Though we don't have staked-out seating in the pavilion, Holly often gravitated toward the center, where she could see and be seen. She was right where I knew she'd be, flanked by Alexis and Belinda—I mean Belle.

This was going to take some maneuvering on my part. The path to Belle took me past Alexis and Holly first. Surely I could not get to her without comment. The path of least resistance would take me around the perimeter of the pavilion and require me to wind through some tables to get to her. It wasn't a difficult choice. I started on the route along the wall when Belle did something entirely unexpected. She waved to me . . . And beckoned me over to her.

The only person more surprised by this than me? Alexis. And Holly. Which I guess would be the only *two* people more surprised by this than me.

I made my way over to the table, feeling like I was walking the gauntlet or the plank or any number of things that mean I was walking to my doom. But then things got even worse when I reached the table and Belle said, "You want to sit with us?"

Conversations halted. People at the tables around us froze. A small child somewhere started crying. But most notably: there was a seismic shift in the class status. I always used to think we didn't have cliques at Orion. That we all hated one another equally and without bias. But that was a lie. With the exception of the Drama Geeks and the Soccer Guys, our cliques were largely undefined and somewhat amorphous, but they were. And when Belle asked me to sit at her table, everyone knew that the walls had just totally come down.

A bit melodramatic? Maybe. But you weren't standing in the center of a largely silent lunchroom, so don't judge.

"Um . . ." I said. "Actually, I was hoping you could join me. And Jason. I had a sudden brainstorm and wanted to pitch it to you two."

"Okay," Belle said without glancing to Holly for permission, another seismic shift in hierarchy. She grabbed her tray and followed me across the pavilion, where Jason—who had been pulled out of his script by the unnerving silence—greeted us with a smile.

And if you still think I'm making more out of this than it warrants, I'd just like to point out that all of this occurred without a sarcastic comment or a biting barb from either Holly or Alexis.

"What's up?" Jason asked as we sat with him.

"I had a thought," I said. "I don't know why I didn't realize this earlier." Well, I did know, but that didn't matter. "I've spent a lot of time with Belle focusing on how her character, Rachel, feels about the fear of being alone. And the loneliness that runs through Hope's plot. And, Jason, I've spent a lot of time working on the passion that Mackenzie feels for Felicia. But we haven't explored the love that you still feel for Belle . . . I mean Rachel. The only way this love triangle is going to resonate with the audience is if they actually believe that there's still some love in your relationship. Mackenzie leaving Rachel needs to be heart wrenching for the audience."

"Yeah," Jason agreed. "I thought I've been tapping into that."

"Oh, you have," I quickly said. No reason to make my actors insecure. "Both of you have. It's just . . . I think we can make more out of it. You two should spend some time together outside of rehearsal. Get to know each other better. That kind of familiarity will come through onstage."

Yeah, I didn't need to suggest that to Belle twice. She was eager to give Method acting a try. My plan was brilliant for its simplicity.

"I'll leave you two," I said. "So that you can . . . bond."

I'm not sure if they were acting, but to judge by the way they were gazing at each other when I left, I suspected that there might have been one less thing for me to worry about.

Kismet

"Don't bother putting up the sign," I told Gary as he pulled the "Closed Rehearsal" posting from his book bag. "Hope is coming by to work on those new lines for the opening of the play," I said. "And Suze wants to check out some things for the costumes. Besides, I'm pretty sure that Eric won't be dropping in and Belle said something about Alexis having an appointment with some *other* famous stylist. So we shouldn't have too much of an audience. Oh, and Drew said he wanted to bring his painting by." I looked to the closed doors at the back of the auditorium. "Where is he, anyway? He said he'd be early."

Little did I suspect, he was there all the time waiting for his cue. As soon as the words were out of my mouth, trumpets blared and the curtains began to part. I honestly should have wondered why they were shut in the first place, since they're usually left open during the day. But once they started opening, I knew exactly what was going on. It was Drew's unveiling.

As the mysterious music continued to herald the big event, I turned my attention to the stage and waited for the painting to be revealed. By the house lights peeking in through the curtain, I saw something hanging center stage. It was difficult to make out since the stage lights weren't on, but as more and more of the light came in, I saw that it was an object the size of the canvas he'd been painting on. Once the curtains were fully open, it was clear that it was Drew's grand creation.

Except that it was hidden under a sheet.

"Well, *that* was anticlimactic," I called out.

Drew stepped onto the stage carrying an iPod boom box that was the source of the prerecorded trumpets. "Yeah. I couldn't figure out how to work the lights."

I shook my head. "Gary?"

"On it," he said, running to the light board.

"Why didn't you just peek out from behind the curtain and ask for help?" I called up to Drew.

He looked at me like the suggestion was insane. "I wanted it to be a surprise."

I turned back to the covered painting. "That it is."

"You ready?" Gary yelled from the light board.

"Drew?" I asked.

"Bring up the lights," Drew called back, replaying the music.

The house lights went down and the stage lights came up.

It wasn't the official show lighting, but the basic light grid would give us a good idea of how the painting would appear on show night. As long as none of the lights fell from the grid and killed us before then.

Hey, it's happened before. Well, not the killing part, but . . .

"Are you ready for the unveiling?" Drew asked.

"I'm standing here, at the edge of the stage, under the proper lighting, and giving you my undivided attention," I said. "Yes! I'm ready for the unveiling."

"If you're going to be all agitated, you are in the wrong mood to view the painting," he said. "We will have to wait until you calm down." He stopped the music and tapped his toe as if he intended to be there awhile.

"Show me the damn painting!" I yelled.

"That's not the proper mood," he said, throwing in a tsk-tsk just to make me madder.

"What's the holdup?" Gary asked as he joined me at the foot of the stage.

"Drew's being Drew," I said, trying to stay mad in spite of how cute Drew looked playing like he didn't want me to see the painting even though clearly he was dying to show me.

What he forgot was that he was playing with the master.

"You're right," I said to him. "I am in the wrong mood to see this. Maybe we should wait. Leave it covered. I'll check it out tomorrow."

"You don't think I'll walk away right now and take it with me?" he asked.

"I know you will," I replied. "But that won't make me see it anytime sooner. So the question is who wants it more? How badly do you think I want to see it? How badly do you want me to see it?"

"Should I go download the *Jeopardy!* theme on this thing?" Drew asked.

"Go right ahead," I replied. "I'll keep guard over the painting while you work on that."

"This is getting annoying," Gary said as he hopped up onstage and ripped the cover off the painting, without musical accompaniment.

It was . . . stunning.

I'd seen the beginnings of the piece only a day before, but that couldn't prepare me for the final product. Drew took my suggestion to heart about adding color. But like everything else in the work, it was subtle. He used shades of blue to lighten the shadows. Green for accent colors. And the slightest dash of red to intensify the differences between the three distinct sections of the painting.

But that wasn't all. I don't know how he managed it, but there was an odd effect under the stage lights. The colors he used had a glossy consistency, where the blacks, whites, and grays were matte. Certain sections of the painting popped more, making it almost three dimensional. The artwork pulled you in and dared you to look away.

"That's what I was talking about," I said, but not in an "I told you so" way. The awe in my voice was clearly evident. Here's someone who walked away from his talent for years. Didn't study. Didn't practice. And he was better than some of the modern masters my mom had a tendency to drag me out to see against my will from time to time.

Drew walked to the edge of the stage and hunched down so he could talk to me without yelling. "You were right," he said. "This would never have happened . . . this wouldn't have come out of me . . . you were right."

I guess we were kind of staring at that point. But not at the artwork. It was one thing to act like friends again. We'd hung out over the summer. Had some good conversations. Been there for each other at times. But that connection that we used to have . . . the bond that we shared since birth . . . it was finally back.

I wasn't the only one who felt it.

"Good job," Gary said, reminding us that we weren't alone. "It's going to look great in the play."

"We'll have to rework the staging," I said immediately. "Bring the picture into it more. I don't want it full-on center. Too distracting. Make it slightly right of center. And light it. Subtle. I don't want it to overwhelm. People shouldn't be distracted by it."

"If we do that, we're going to have to move the couch to balance out the scene," Gary said.

"Do it," I said. "It's only a minor adjustment to the staging. The cast can handle it."

"Really," Drew said. "You're making more out of this than—"

"Drew," I said. "People are going to see this painting and start a bidding war in the middle of the play." My eyes went wide. "That's it! Drew. How many more paintings can you do by Saturday?"

Drew hesitated. "I don't know. A couple?"

"You're going to need more than a couple," I said. "A lot more. We're going to put them out in the lobby. Make it a showcase for your art. We've got two intermissions. People are going to need something to look at. Just don't make them as good as this one. I want to save that for the play."

"How am I supposed to make them not as good as this one?"

"Don't bother me with detail questions," I said like the decisive director I am. "Just do it. I'll arrange everything with Mr. Randall."

What a great idea, if I do say so myself. Now Drew would have an entire series to include in his portfolio *and* his own show to brag about to whatever school he decided to apply to. Granted, it would be fairly useless if he ultimately decided to study accounting, but it was a start. I couldn't hold his hand all the way through the admissions process.

Could I?

Drew dropped down beside me and pulled me away from Gary. "Seriously. If you're suggesting this to be nice—"

"When have I ever been nice to you?" I asked.

He didn't have time to answer because Hope came running down the aisle. "Holy crap!" she screamed, ever the demur one in the group. "Did you do that? It's more perfect than I imagined. I can't believe you never let me see this side of you when we were dating, you moron. I'm freakin' speechless!"

For someone speechless she sure had a lot to say. And she was saying it quite loudly. When she stopped yelling, Hope pulled him into a smothering hug, crushing him under the weight of her impressive breasts.

"That is seriously some beautiful artwork," Sam agreed with less enthusiasm but equal artistic appreciation.

"Amazing!" Suze gushed, completing the trio of new arrivals.

"Thank you," Drew said once Hope released him. He was being all adorably shy, but I could tell he was basking in the love.

The ego stroking only got better a minute later when Jason and Belle came into the auditorium. Together. And I wasn't the only one who noticed.

"You okay?" I asked Sam while the rest of the group chatted up Drew about his previously hidden talent.

"Why wouldn't I be?" she asked genuinely. Like she didn't have a clue what I was talking about. And, okay, Jason and Belle had only walked in together. It wasn't like they were holding hands or laughing over a shared joke or anything like that. And Sam didn't have a clue about my scheme to get them together so her relationship with Eric would be safe. But still, she had been watching Jason and Belle the entire time they came down the long aisle to the stage.

"No reason," I said as we all turned back to the painting to admire it some more before we got the rehearsal started. Which is why we didn't notice when the group grew by one until a voice behind us said, "Not bad."

Shock was evident on several faces as we turned to see Eric

holding out his fist to pound against Drew's as he said, "Dude."

No wonder he left it to me to have the serious conversations if all he could come up with was "Not bad" followed by "Dude" to express his emotions after viewing his best friend's moving artwork.

"It's okay that I'm here?" Eric asked me for some reason. "I didn't see the sign on the door."

Knowing better, I turned the question over to Sam.

"It's great," she said. Seeing this as an opening—because why else would he be here if it wasn't for her?—Sam grabbed him and pulled him away from the crowd.

"Gary, please make the changes to the set we were talking about and we can get into opening positions," I said to give everyone something to do so they weren't all focused on Sam and Eric. Then I went over to my seat so I could go through some notes in my director's prompt book.

Is it my fault that Sam had taken Eric over to that same part of the auditorium to talk?

Is it my fault that I stuck around, making myself look busy, so I could eavesdrop?

Okay, one of those things kind of was my fault. But you'd think my best friend would know me better than that and go farther away.

"No," Sam said. "I'm sorry."

Darn, I missed the opening of their reunion.

"I should have figured it would be . . . weird seeing me kiss another guy," she said. "We should have talked about it first."

"Well, you did give me Hope's play to read," he said. "I should have gotten around to it before . . . you know. Besides, I know you don't like Jason. It's just stupid jealousy. I trust you completely."

"Oh," she said. I worried that he was the only one involved in the conversation who trusted her.

"Hear anything interesting?" Drew asked in my ear, causing me to drop my prompt book.

"Thanks," I said, leaving it on the ground.

"No, thank you," he said with a nod back to his painting. "Does . . . um . . . does this mean I get a hyphen?"

"What?"

"A hyphen," he said. "A hyphenate. Whatever you call it when you give people titles based on what they do. I'm the only person you know who you never gave a hyphenate to. I get that it's because I don't have any real talents or anything, but . . . I heard you even gave Eric a hyphenate."

"Yeah, but one of his titles was 'asshat' so it's nothing to be jealous of."

"Still," he said. "I'd kind of like one."

"What did you have in mind?"

"I was thinking something like painter–sucky soccer player."

I wanted to laugh, but there seemed to be genuine hurt in his tone. Like I'd been intentionally ignoring him all this time. Still, I couldn't agree to his hyphenate and let him think so little of his abilities. "Drew, I would never call you that. From now on, to me, you're *artist*–sucky soccer player, okay?"

"Okay," he said, and then we actually pounded fists. "I should get to work on those paintings."

"You can stick around for rehearsal if you want," I said. "You've got four days. I could dash off a dozen paintings in that time."

"You do realize it is a bit more work than slapping some paint on a canvas?"

"You do realize I was just kidding?" I said.

"We going to get to work, boss?" Gary interrupted, with a bit more emphasis on the word "boss" than normal, and Drew took that as his cue to leave. Seeing how Hope already had her notebook out, Suze had her sketchbook, Jason and Belle were already in position, and Sam was wasting time kissing Eric, I figured it was time to get down to business.

Applause

"What is Mr. Randall doing here?" Belinda asked the following afternoon with a quivering voice that no director likes to hear.

"He asked to sit in on our run-through," I explained.

"Doesn't he have his own rehearsal?" she asked.

"Jimmy's running it," I said. Now, Jimmy Wilkey running a rehearsal on his own is something I wished I could see. He probably had the actors doing calisthenics to warm up. Maybe a brisk five-mile hike.

"Why didn't you warn us he was coming?" she asked.

Seeing Belinda Connors stressing out and so insecure a couple weeks ago would have been fodder for hours of entertainment for me and my friends. Two days ago it would have been adorably sweet. But five minutes before we ran through my directorial debut for our teacher . . . well, it was a concern. "He's only here to help," I assured her. "Not to judge. But that doesn't matter, because I know we're going to impress him. And you in particular are going to make him wish you'd auditioned for him before senior year."

That got a smile of relief. From her. I was still freaking out. This was our last day in the auditorium before we had to turn it back over to Mr. Randall and Ms. Monroe to split for Thursday's rehearsal. The next time we were scheduled for stage time was Friday. And that was going to be tech. (*Aside:* "Tech" or "technical rehearsal" is when we figure out the lighting and sound and backstage issues. Any of the myriad things we theater people use to augment the actors' performances. We also discuss things that could go wrong at any point during the show: the stage being thrown into darkness, the sound system screeching with feedback, people running into one another backstage.)

For tech I turn the rehearsal over to the stage manager (and associate stage manager). This rehearsal was going to be my last chance to work with my actors onstage and I had to do it in front of my teacher. Mr. Randall had said that he was only there for support, but I couldn't help feeling like this was a final exam. Like if I failed, he'd either take over as director or cut the play from the festival. Not that he could have done either without parental backlash from several fronts, but that's why someone coined the term "irrational fear."

I left my cast backstage and joined Mr. Randall in a row around the middle of Hall Hall. The usual assortment of friends were gathered in the front row, minus Drew, who was busy in the art studio. I'd skipped the kiss again the day before, so Eric hadn't had to sit through it. I couldn't do that today. Even though Sam assured me he was now fine with it, I couldn't help worrying that things would be different when he saw it today, watching from the first row.

I didn't have to worry for long, though, as I soon had many other thoughts occupying my mind. I'd promised my cast I would try to let them run through the play without interruption. After Gary gave Belle the opening cue, I immediately regretted that promise.

Not that my cast wasn't excellent. They were. But they weren't perfect. There were little things I wanted to change throughout the rehearsal. Belle's nerves had exhibited themselves with a brief bout of chicken necking when she first stepped onstage. Sam and Jason got so into the emotion of the scene at one point that they forgot a chunk of the blocking. And all three of them stumbled over a line at various points. None of it was major, but it wasn't quite perfection.

Mr. Randall understood what was going on in my mind, because he pulled me back into my seat several times during the run-through. I'd only been on the edge. I hadn't stood yet. But each time, he gave me a smile and whispered, "Let them go."

Five minutes into the play, Mr. Randall handed me a notepad so I could start jotting down things to work on. The problem was every time I wrote something, I had to look down at the page, and I worried that I was missing something else that needed to be tweaked. I finally stopped looking down and just wrote blindly. At one point I glanced at the page and saw an indecipherable mess. But still, I didn't stop the performance.

It was hard. Impossible, even. I couldn't imagine what it was going to be like show night. To be sitting in the audience with no control over what happened onstage. Sure, I had a taste of it when I directed a short scene during the Summer Theatrical Program. But this was different.

It was longer for one thing. Not as much as a full-length play, but still bigger than a scene. It was also going to be performed in front of a paying audience. Okay, not a *paying* audience, but an audience that pays for their children to go to Orion Academy, which costs *way* more than tickets to a Broadway show.

Having to be in the audience of my show with a half dozen other people without being able to comment was bad enough. But I got through it. Several times I even got lost in the production and enjoyed it along with everyone around me. Then something small would happen—like when Belle dropped a flower on the ground and nobody bothered to pick it up for the rest of the play!—and I'd go right into director mode, jotting down illegible notes.

Until we got to the end.

I should have been watching the stage. I should have been paying attention to my actors. But my interest went right to Eric.

From the corner of my eye, I saw Sam and Jason go in for the kiss. Their movements matched exactly what they had done on Monday. The intensity was there. The emotion was raw. And I wasn't even experiencing it full-on. My mind—and eyes—were elsewhere.

Eric didn't react. He remained leaning back in his chair, relaxed, as if nothing were going on. I couldn't see his face, but Gary could from his position at the foot of the stage. Ever the observant associate stage manager, he caught my eye and gave a shrug that I took to mean Eric's lack of interest was the same from the front as it was from the back.

I couldn't say the rest of the audience had the same reaction.

It was the first time the kiss was performed in front anyone other than me . . . and Eric. The first time Hope had seen the full culmination of her play. Her words brought to full chromatic life. Not that I could see the look on her face since she was sitting in the front row. But I couldn't have missed her reaction even if I had been focused on the stage. As soon as Sam grabbed on to Jason and pulled him into the kiss, both Hope and Suze leaned forward. It was almost comical how they did it in unison. But it wasn't funny at all. The moment had drawn them into the play. Literally.

The room was hushed as Gary hopped up and pulled the curtain closed.

Hope led the applause. She was up on her feet before the curtain had reopened. We hadn't rehearsed a curtain call yet, so it was the cast just kind of standing there. They all took sort of halfhearted bows as everyone joined Hope, standing as well.

Hope even turned to applaud me, and I swear I saw her green eyes welling with tears.

"Bravo! Brava!" I called to the stage, then to the playwright, "Author! Author." Then I picked up my notepad. "I've got notes!"

What? We'd have time to celebrate later. The show went up in three days and we still had work to do.

While the cast came down and basked in the attention of the small audience, I turned to Mr. Randall to get his take on things. The man who tends to gush over the smallest student break-throughs was unusually stoic, which scared the hell out of me. Was it so bad that he couldn't even act like he was entertained?

"There were some very nice things taking place onstage," he said without any show of emotion.

That's it? That's what I get?

"Yeah, but it's not there yet," I said, holding up my scribbled notes. I wanted it to be clear that I was willing to work this thing day and night until Saturday. If he would just give me some indication of what was wrong. "I get that. I'd love your take on things. Any suggestions?"

"You should work on everything you wrote down on your notepad during the rehearsal," he said. Big help.

"That's it?"

"Oh, and yes," he said, breaking into a smile, "it was so much further along than I thought it would be. Bryan, you did an amazing job. I knew letting you direct was a good decision, but I never imagined you would come through so brilliantly."

I'm not afraid to say there were some tears . . . welling . . . in the corner of my right eye. I was *not* crying. "Well, you have to say that," I joked to break the mood. *My* mood. "You're afraid of losing your job if you upset me."

"True," he said with a laugh. "But I'm not required to do this. Ms. Monroe and I agreed that if your run through was where we hoped it would be, we would close the festival with *Achromantic*. Save the best for last. What I saw surpassed my expectations. You get the spotlight position."

Speechless.

That's what I was. Which is saying something for me.

Every student wanted to be in the last play of the festival. It was the one the audience walked out remembering. Usually the spot went to the celebrity guest director. I never dared to imagine that I would get it.

Once the room stopped spinning, my teacher/mentor made a few suggestions, which I quickly wrote down. His comments were fairly minimal. It's a good thing too, because my hands were shaking so much from the excitement that my handwriting was worse than when I was making notes without looking at the page.

Mr. Randall gave another round of applause to the cast, then left to join his rehearsal so I could go over my notes. But first I had to share the news.

The cheer that came from everyone echoed through the school. The only person who didn't seem overjoyed, oddly enough, was Sam.

"Take ten," I told everyone. "Go grab some snacks from the machines in the pavilion. But, Sam, can I see you real quick?"

She was confused but waved Eric away to go get snackage and came over to me. Once the auditorium cleared out, I asked her what was wrong.

"Nothing," she replied, like there was any chance I was going to believe her.

"Try again," I said.

"You're not going to understand," she said.

"Make me."

"You're *really* not going to understand," she said.

If we were going to have another conversation about how I can't give her advice because I've never known the love of another person, I swear I was going to kill her. Dead. In the middle of the auditorium.

Well, maybe I'd wait until after the One-Act Festival.

"Sam!"

"You were probably watching the kiss at the end of the play," she said.

"My attention was kind of divided," I admitted. "I may also have been watching Eric for a reaction."

"So you saw," she said. "I mean, I was onstage, so I couldn't tell entirely. But you saw him."

"Sam, there's nothing to worry about," I assured her. "He was fine with it. He didn't react at all."

"That's exactly what I mean!" she said. "It didn't bother him. Not at all. Don't you think it's a little odd, since he was so upset the other day? And now, *nothing*. No reaction. It's like he doesn't care. Something happened. Something happened that he's not telling me about."

I paused to take in what she was saying. Then I gave her my brightest smile. "See!" I said. "I totally understand. You're a freakin' lunatic!"

Thoroughly Modern Millie
or
Much Ado About Nothing

Sam's sanity was totally absent for the next couple days. Every time I saw her, she quizzed me on what I thought it meant that Eric was perfectly fine with her kissing another guy. Questions ranged from "How did he get over it so fast?" to "Do you think it's all an act?" to the ever-astonishing "Should I break up with him?"

That was the one that came out over the phone one hour before we were supposed to be at school on the night of the Fall One-Act Festival. It was also the one that did me in. "I'm hanging up now," I said. And I did.

Did I really have to deal with this on the night of the damn show? Because I was so not in the mood. There was already too much on my mind.

Sam's psychosis aside, the past few days had been great . . . excellent even. We'd spent the rest of Wednesday afternoon working on my notes. Thursday was mainly cleanup stuff in

Anne's room. And Friday was tech. During tech we all got out of class for the day and ran the full Fall One-Act Festival twice. In the morning we stopped and started our way through all the technical aspects of the show. And in the afternoon we did a nonstop dress rehearsal.

The morning tech was nightmarish, as they always are. But the afternoon dress was a sight to behold. Everything that could have gone right did. From Belle's offstage opening to the kiss to end all kisses, the production was pitch-perfect.

See why I was a mess?

There's an old theater adage that basically goes "If you have a bad dress rehearsal, it means you'll have a good show." Well, we'd had an *amazing* dress rehearsal. So naturally, by the time I was getting ready to leave Saturday night for the show, I was a nervous wreck. My hands were seriously shaking as I tried to tie my tie. I eventually gave up, figuring an open-collar thing was always in fashion.

I did look sharp (that's a Blaine word) in my skinny black jeans, cobalt blue dress shirt, and my usual fedora, which was slanted in a devil-may-care manner that *so* did not match my mood. But a pair of cameos—one expected, one a total surprise—were about to go a long way in lightening my mood.

"Knockety knock knock," a voice sang with the matching sound of accompanying knocks. Yes, it was childish. And a bit girly even, but there was no girl at my bedroom door. And, no, it was not one of my gay friends, so don't even go there with the stereotypes.

"Dad!" I sprang across the room to the door as he swung it

open . . . right into my shoulder. It should have been a sign, but I was too excited about seeing my dad, who had been out of the country fighting terrorists for the past three weeks. (At least, that's what I like to think he does. It's so much more exciting than his real job . . . whatever that is.)

"Sorry about that," he said, wrapping me in a hug, careful of the bruise that was surely growing on my shoulder. "But I picked up a surprise at the airport that might make the pain more bearable."

"Presents?" I said, reverting back to five years old. "Shiny new toys!"

"Well, neither shiny, new, nor a toy," he said. "But your grandma is in the kitchen."

"Grandma Millie!" I shouted as I forgot all about Dad and ran to Grandma. Dad had only been MIA three weeks. Grandma had been touring the world for months. I couldn't imagine the presents she brought me!

I raced through the house to find Mom already pouring Grandma a scotch in the kitchen. It's incredible, but the older Grandma gets, the more she looks like Mom's sister rather than her mother. I can only hope, wish, dream, and beg whoever is listening that I inherit that trait. Not that I want to look like my mom's sister, but . . . you know what I mean.

I hurried to her, but she held out a hand, stopping me dead in my tracks. "I refuse to hug you while you're wearing that asinine hat."

"But," I said, "it was Grandpa's."

"Damn right," she said, removing my fedora—an act that

usually resulted in death. "You should never wear anything older than you are. I hated that thing when your grandpa wore it, and I hate it even more on you." Before I could stop her, she walked over to the trash can, stepped on the foot pedal to open the lid, and . . . dropped my fedora on top of a pile of coffee grounds. Then she turned back to me with her arms out wide. "Come to Grandma and give her some sugar," she said sweetly.

I couldn't move. My fedora was in the trash.

My fedora was *in the trash!*

Seeing me frozen, Grandma Millie came to me and wrapped me in her own hug. Too bad she didn't know to avoid the bruised shoulder. "Ouch!" I said.

"That's okay, honey," she replied. "Sometimes love hurts." While she clamped on to me, my eyes never left the trash can. All my parents could do was shrug. If any of us removed the fedora from the trash, Grandma would just pick it back up, dust it off, and throw it out all over again. She's a determined old broad. And she'd be the first to tell you that.

In case you're wondering, it's not that we're afraid of Grandma. It's just that we know that against her we'll never win. And to be honest, we're usually okay with that. Besides, I could always fish the fedora out of the trash later, after she'd gone to bed. We had a show to get to.

"Wait," Grandma said as she mussed my hair. "There. Much better." I snuck a peek in the reflection on the shiny metal above the stove. What can I say? She was right. My hair looked pretty good. Maybe it was time to stop hiding it underneath the fedora.

"Let's go get some grub," Grandma said, slapping me on the shoulder. Maybe she did know about the bruise.

"Grub?" I asked, finally managing the successful raising of one eyebrow.

"Don't make a face like that," she said. "It might stick that way."

"How grandmotherly of you," I said, which was so *unlike* her.

"Learned my lesson," she replied. "If it wasn't for all the plastic surgery, my own face would look like this." She screwed up her expression to look rather like a gargoyle statue I had up in my room.

"Like you've ever been under the knife," I said as she downed her scotch in one gulp and we all headed out to the car.

"Well, one time back in the fifties I was in a knife fight," she said. "Does that count?"

On the way to the restaurant, she shared the harrowing tale of a particularly bloody prison rumble she took part in. Seeing how she was never in her life even close to a prison, we all enjoyed it for the tall tale that it was.

We met up with Blaine at Gladstone's on the Beach for dinner, where Grandma moved on to share even more exciting stories of her travels abroad. In light of the prison escapade, you can understand if we were skeptical about the truth in those stories. Actually, Mom was hoping they were more lies than anything else. We were getting a fairly detailed telling of Grandma's adventure running with the bulls in Pamplona when they dropped me off at school.

Then they went off to have dessert without me!

Even though *Achromantic* was the last show in the festival, the cast's call time was one hour before curtain. Technically, as the director, I didn't have to be there early. My job was done. I could sit back, relax (ha!), and bask in the praise of a job well done. Or at least drown my worries in some chocolate cake with my family. But, no. I had to be there to support my actors.

The things a director gives up for his cast.

I got the distinct impression that my evening wasn't going to be quite that kicked back when Gary came running up to me the moment I walked in the door. He was all frantic and agitated, looking way more like Jimmy Wilkey on show night than I ever thought possible. (Note to self: Never be a stage manager. It's not good for the mental health.)

"Thank *God* you're here!" he shouted frantically as he dragged me along with him.

It's always nice to be wanted, but . . . "What's wrong?" I asked in horror, hurrying with Gary through the halls. I barely had the time to notice that Drew's artwork had been hung in the lobby, much less stop to admire it.

"I was heading to the office to find some electrical tape," he said. "It's supposed to be in the stage manager's box, but there wasn't any. I didn't expect you here so early, but I am *so glad* to see you. We're having a teeny-tiny emergency in the dressing room." Funny how Gary wasn't acting like it was that teeny or tiny of an emergency.

Gary rushed me into the dressing room, where I found Suze mending a rather large gash in Belle's dress while the actress was still wearing it. "And what's going on here?" I asked.

"Minor accident with a random nail," Suze said calmly. "I'll have it patched up in a snap."

Gary slumped a bit, his agitation leaving him. "Suze wasn't here when I went for the electrical tape," he said. "Guess I panicked a smidge."

I preferred to ignore the idea that my associate stage manager was about to tape an actress into her wardrobe, and focus on the issue at hand. Before things got out of hand. So I grabbed Gary by the hand and pulled him to the side. "What's up? I've never seen you freak out like this before any other show. And during *Wizard* you were doing stunts onstage."

"That's acting," he said. "I can handle the onstage stuff. It's the backstage stuff I'm worried about. I've never run a show before. I mean, I know Jimmy is handling the light and sound cues, but once you go out and take your seat, the cast is my responsibility. I tell them where to go and what to do. What if I blow their calls for curtain?"

"Then I will come back here and kill you," I said with mock seriousness. Well, maybe it was only a *little* mock.

This clearly did not make him any less stressed.

"Gary, you're going to be fine," I said. "And even if you're not, you're working with a cast of experienced actors. Or . . . well . . . maybe not Belle, but she's good at following direction. Just look at how much her sister and Holly tell her to do in a given day. It's going to be fine."

Cue the crisis.

Sam came up to me all panicky. "We lost Drew's painting."

"WHAT?" I looked to my associate stage manager for an explanation.

Now he seemed calm. "It's okay," he said. "Jimmy was worried about it since it's so important to the play. He put it someplace safe."

"Yeah," Sam said. "He can't remember where he put it. And he's too afraid to tell you both."

"Jimmy!" Gary yelled.

I grabbed him before he could do any damage. "That's not how to do it," I said. "Sam, where is he?"

"Backstage."

I did my best to calm myself as I left the dressing room and went to the stage. Jimmy was in hyper mode, rummaging through every pile of junk that was stuck out of the way in the wings since we'd run out of space in the storage room.

"Jimmy," I said softly so I didn't give him a heart attack. "I'm here to help."

"Bryan! I'm so sorry. I didn't mean . . . I don't remember . . . it's just, there's been so much going on this week that—"

"It's okay, Jimmy," I said in the most soothing tone I could muster. If we couldn't find the painting, I'm sure there was another one in Drew's collection on display in the lobby that we could use. Maybe there'd even be something as perfect as the one he painted specifically for the show. I hoped.

"But Mr. Randall's always saying—"

"What a great stage manager you are." I supplied him with a sentence he clearly hadn't been going for himself.

"You're just a little too organized. Now, I want you to think about the painting. You wouldn't have put it someplace we couldn't get to it. You would put it somewhere perfect, where none of us would ever look even though it's the most obvious place in the world."

Circuitous logic was Jimmy's specialty. All you had to do was speak his language. Apparently, I'd translated correctly, because he got that spark of recognition in his eyes and looked up above us.

Knowing better than to question anything Jimmy did, I looked up too. Drew's painting was hanging in the rafters. Jimmy had rigged it to the fly system so he could store it above the stage.

"All we have to do is drop it down during intermission," he said proudly and with a tremendous amount of relief.

"Very smart," I said, patting him on the back before returning to my cast.

I reassured everyone that the painting was safe and told Gary exactly where it was in case there was a repeat episode while I was out front with the audience. Seeing how I'd already had my fill of emergencies, I figured it was time to go check on the attendance, even though there was a while till curtain. If another emergency came up, I was sure Gary would come find me.

"I'm going around front," I told Gary. "But first, if I could have a few words with my cast."

Sam, Jason, and Belle extricated themselves from the various conversations they were in with the members of other casts and joined me in the corner of the dressing room with Gary. There were so many things I wanted to say to them. About how much they'd impressed me over the past few weeks. About how I was sure the show was going to be a total success. So many thoughts were going through my head that I couldn't manage to put them in order. Which is why all that came out of my mouth was, "Break a leg."

Not the most inspirational of speeches, I know.

When it became clear that nothing else would be coming, Sam said, "You too."

Then we all went back to business.

I went out to the front lobby to see if my parents were back from dessert yet. They'd only gone down the road to the Cupcake Emporium, but even a small dessert like that would take more time than I'd been there dealing with the minor crises.

I was right, of course. My parents weren't back yet. But the gathering crowd was already pretty impressive. The Fall One-Act Festival was always standing room only, which is why so many people had come out early. Good thing my family had seats specially reserved in the front row.

Even though I couldn't find my folks, I did see someone pushing through the crowd making a beeline for me. I couldn't tell who it was at first, then I couldn't *believe* who it was when she reached me.

Hope was standing in front of me in a green blouse, beige Capri pants, a chunky green and brown necklace, and a pair of sparkly green platform wedges, carrying an orange purse.

The traditional Goth-Ick look of all black with a touch of color was gone. Even her natural hazel eyes were staring back at me, instead of her colored contacts.

I didn't need to ask. Hope saw the question in my eyes.

"Turns out my therapist was right," she admitted. "I'd been hiding behind my Goth-Ick armor, not letting anyone see the true me that I only expressed through my writing."

"Deep," I said with understanding.

"Did you make the same connection with your fedora?" she asked, pointing to my unhatted head.

"My grandma threw it out," I said meekly.

She smiled. "Whatever works. So . . . how you doing?"

"I want to throw up," I replied. "You?"

"I just did," she said. "Mint?" she held out an Altoids tin. I gladly took one. The bile in my stomach was churning and I was hoping the curiously strong peppermint would help settle it.

It didn't.

She put the tin back in her bag and pulled out a program. "Here. Grabbed you one. For your collection."

"Thanks," I said. I hadn't seen the program since Gary went over the preliminary design with me. It was so exciting. I opened the program and scanned down to the third play on the list. *Achromantic.*

Beneath the title, in big, bold letters, it said: "Director."

And beside that: "Brian Stark."

Sigh.

Love! Valour! Compassion!

My name being spelled wrong in the program wasn't
the last crisis of the evening. Not that a misspelling was a crisis, but it was darn annoying. My name has been spelled with
an "i" instead of a "y" in about half the programs I've ever been
in. That, I was used to. But this time I was the director. I had
final approval of the layout before it went to the printers.
"Bryan" had been spelled correctly back then. *How does that
happen?*

I'd wanted to ask Gary about it each of the times he ran out
to the lobby to update me on the latest problem. But seeing
how he was already overreacting to even the smallest things,
I didn't want to add to his grief.

"Bryan, the flowers are wilted!"

"Bryan, Belinda let Alexis touch her hair!"

"Bryan, the stage collapsed killing all the actors!"

"Run that one by me again?" I asked.

"Just seeing if I can get a reaction," he said. "Why are you so calm when I'm going nuts?"

"Because I have given up all control of the play," I said, in a Zen-like state. "I have given it to *you*, which is probably why you're nuts, but there is nothing I can do now. It is in my actors' hands. And yours. So I am going to relax. Chat with people. And admire Drew's fine artwork with Hope. Sound good, Hope?"

"Sounds excellent," she replied.

He regarded us like we were both crazy. "What is this, like, costume night? Why aren't you two dressed normal with the hat and the black?"

"We are not dressed normal, because we *aren't* normal," I said. I don't know if the stuff I was spewing was actually Zen in any way, but it didn't matter. Gary shook his head and left us for the last time.

"Where's Drew?" I asked as Hope and I examined another piece in the Drew Campbell collection. He'd managed a half dozen paintings in the past few days. None of them was quite as spectacular as the one we were using in the play, but they were all better than anything I'd ever seen done by a high school student. He stayed in the theme of black and white with a dash of color so the collection was cohesive, but each painting had a different feel. I didn't know if he was getting serious about art school, but with his talent I was fairly sure he'd be a lock for the better schools in the country. Preferably those on the West Coast.

"You know how Gary's being about the play?" she said.

"Drew's the same way about people seeing his artwork for the first time. Eric's in the auditorium saving him a seat so he can slip in at the last second without anyone cornering him to talk about his art."

"What a spectacular idea," I said. "Think anyone would notice if we disappeared?"

"Probably," Hope said as we were accosted by the head-master's wife.

People had been coming up to us all evening to talk about how exciting it was that we were putting on a student-produced play for the first time in Orion history. Not all the parents were quite as enthusiastic about it. Neither were all the former students. Of particular note was Holly Mayflower's sister, who'd been forced to fly in from college for the week-end to attend.

Heather Mayflower's reaction was to look Hope and me up and down and say, "It's a shame how the drama program has declined here since I left."

Our response? We laughed in her face.

Hope's mother saved us by making her grand entrance. Mrs. Ellis had flown in from New York for the production, which is typical for our larger school events. My father wasn't the only one who made sure he didn't miss his child's moments in the spotlight. Following the mother/daughter reunion, I watched the fun of Hope bringing her mom over to say hi to her dad and stepmom. It was as entertaining as always. Don't get me wrong. Hope's mom and dad got along better than most married parents, but Hope's stepmom and her ridiculous insecurity make any reunion a joy to behold.

My parents showed up a few minutes later with Grandma and Blaine. The two of them were comparing imaginary scars, one-upping each other on the exciting ways they had gotten them. When he reached me, Blaine mussed my hair even more than it already was.

"My kingdom for a fedora," I said, swiping his hands away.

"You ready?" he asked.

"Not even," I said.

"Aw, but the hard part is done," he said.

But he was wrong. So very wrong.

The lights in the lobby flickered, gently suggesting that we should get the hell into our seats. Like lemmings, we all followed the instructions. Hope even grasped on to my hand as we entered. There were two plays to perform before ours, but we'd finally reached the point of no return. No turning back. Short of yelling "Fire!" in the crowded theater, there was no way to stop it. I wondered where the nearest fire alarm was located. It wouldn't be the first time I'd debated throwing a false alarm to get me out of the inevitable.

"Weird being on this side of things," Hope said as we shuffled down the aisle behind the slower-moving audience members.

"Too right," I said in a random British accent. Like Madonna.

It *was* weird seeing the show from the audience side of things. Right now everyone was making the final preparations backstage. Jimmy was yelling at Ms. Monroe's cast to get in their damn places, even though they probably already were.

My cast would be done with makeup and hair, and sitting in a corner somewhere so they don't get in the way. It was still too early for any of them to be going through their warm-up routines, but that would start shortly. I wanted to be back there with them. Going over last-minute details. Giving that inspiring speech that I couldn't come up with. But Mr. Randall had forced me . . . I mean, he impressed upon me how it was important for the director to be able to let go. To trust his cast and his stage manager. To sit and watch the show, not as an audience member, but as a part of the team. This was my role now. To support my cast.

And to applaud the loudest even if they screw it all up.

I was remembering that part of the conversation as I saw Drew run in and take a seat beside Eric a moment before the lights went down and the curtain opened on the first play.

I'm sure I knew what play Ms. Monroe had chosen at some point over the past couple weeks. It had to be in the program at the very least. But I couldn't tell anyone what was going on in front of me. My mind was too busy going over every last detail of my play. Of Hope's play. Trying to remember any note I had left out. Figure out any scene that still wasn't working. I didn't pay attention to even one minute of the show. All the calmness that Gary had been so envious of before the show was gone. I was a nervous mess.

Before I knew it, the lights were up in the auditorium again. People were mingling, heading back out to the lobby to admire Drew's art and running to the bathrooms. At some point, I think Dad said something to me about Ms. Monroe's play. I might have nodded in response. Maybe there was a grunt. Hope and I were dead to the world.

The audience came back in and the lights went down again. I returned to consciousness somewhere around Holly's big emotional breakdown. Her *character's* emotional breakdown, that is. I had to admit, the girl was good. I can never understand why some actresses who are the best talents onstage are the worst people in real life.

Then again, it's possible I never gave her a chance, like with Belle.

Or . . . maybe not.

Suddenly, Mr. Randall's play was done.

And I realized that something had to be done.

Before the lights were up, I bolted out of my seat, scaring my family around me.

"Be right back," I said, fast-walking up the aisle, trying not to look panicky. I'd forgotten to tell Hope to come with me, but that didn't matter. She was right by my side pushing through the crowd. I nearly stopped when I saw Holly's dad—famous music producer Anthony Mayflower—corner Drew in his seat, but I refused to let my curiosity divert me from my mission.

Once we were out in the lobby, we burst into a run. Considering neither of us was a sprinter, it was surprising how quickly we burst into the drama class, which served as the green room on show night.

Gary and the cast were standing in a circle holding hands in silence. None of them was a particularly praying person;

they were getting connected in the way that every cast I've ever been in likes to do before a show. I waited to give them their moment, but it was broken up early when Jimmy came up behind me and loudly asked, "Bryan, what's wrong?"

All eyes snapped open and turned in my direction.

"Nothing, Jimmy," I said calmly. "I just need a minute with the cast. Gary can give them the five-minute call for places."

"Oh, okay," he said, slightly put out that I wasn't sending Gary away too.

Once Jimmy was gone the cast released hands and turned to give me their full attention.

"I suck at speeches," I said, getting right down to the matter. "Absolutely suck at the inspirational thing. That's why I haven't been doing the whole 'show must go on' shtick through rehearsals. Which is odd, because you all know how I like to talk." This got a smile from everyone. "But I could not let you go out on that stage without letting you all know what this experience has meant to me. I never thought I'd direct anything. Never thought I'd do anything but be one of the people onstage. And I certainly never thought I'd have Belle in any cast of mine." I said that lightly, so that everyone laughed. Okay, Hope let out a huff, but it was much more subdued than normal.

"I've been out in the audience freaking out all night," I continued. "Not because I don't trust you all to give a great performance, because I do. Not because we don't have one of the most amazing scripts ever, because we do. And not because I don't think the show won't run smoothly, because I know

Gary will take control when Jimmy has his inevitable nervous breakdown." That one earned a small laugh. "I was worried that I didn't do my job. That I didn't do enough. That anything that goes wrong will be my fault. And it will. I am your director and it all comes down to me. But that's not entirely true. This is our show. It's not Hope's. It's not mine. It's ours. No matter what craziness was going on around us, we came together and made something real. Something beautiful. And I wanted to thank you all for it."

We all came together in a group hug. In that circle, between Belle and Gary, I felt warm and I felt loved.

Of all people, Jason was the one to break the moment. "So you're saying, if we mess up, it's all on us? That we can't blame you?"

I nodded. "Why else would I come back here and go through all that?"

When we finally broke apart, Sam reached over and pulled me and Hope into a more private hug. It may have been a soupcon on the cliquish side, but we didn't care. We still had seven months of school and one full-scale production to go, but this felt like our graduation. We had taken all our talent to the next level. Sure, there may have been some disagreements along the way, but our friendship was stronger for it.

Once we were done hugging I pulled Sam over to the side. Hope immediately glommed on to Gary because Jason and Belle had their heads together in private conversation.

The first time we were ever in a show together, Sam and I played this game where we tried to do anything we could to throw the other person off before he or she entered the scene. We would try to make the other laugh before an entrance, tie shoelaces together, mess up hair. Stupid stuff. We'd only had small parts, so it wasn't like we were threatening the play. And only one of us managed to shock the other out of character for a brief moment. The game lasted all of one performance before we realized it was immature and thoroughly unprofessional.

But, what the hell? I thought. *Sometimes we all have to be immature and unprofessional.*

"Wonder what's going on there," I said with a nod to Jason and Belle, who were looking way chummy.

"Is it wrong that I'm jealous?" she asked.

I should have thought more about this game before I played it. "Why don't we talk about it after the show?"

"No," she insisted. "I can't go out there with these feelings for Jason. I have to tell him. I have to deal with this now."

"You're messing with me, aren't you?"

She smacked me in my head. Since it wasn't blunted by my fedora, I felt it full-on. "Don't go bringing up things like that before I have to go on!"

"Sorry," I said. "But you are okay, right?"

She sighed. "I don't know. I'm confused. I can't talk about it now."

"I get it."

"Not because you don't know what I'm feeling," she quickly said to spare my feelings. "That was stupid. Just because you've never experienced something doesn't mean you can't give me advice."

For some reason I needed to be honest with Sam in that moment. I needed to tell her the one thing I've never told anyone. *Ever.* I couldn't believe I was going to spring it on her six minutes before curtain, but I didn't feel like I had a choice. And not because of some game we used to play. Though this could make her mess up her entrance.

"About that," I said. "I've been keeping something from you."

"More secrets?" she asked. "Didn't we do this once before?"

"It wasn't my secret," I explain. "Not mine alone, I mean. You see, I have been kissed. *Really* kissed. Not some spin the bottle thing with Suze when we were twelve. I mean, a real actual boy-on-boy kiss."

I got the reaction I'd been expecting. Her whole body jumped back in surprise. "What? When? How? And why the hell didn't you tell me?" That last question came with another smack. By the time the evening was over, I was going to be bruised over half my body.

"It happened before I met you," I said. "The day of Grandpa's funeral. I was a wreck. Inconsolable. When we got back to the house for the reception, my parents let me go straight to my room. I didn't want to talk to anyone. I just wanted to cry."

"I didn't realize you two were so close," she said. "I mean, I know you loved him and all, but I never . . ."

"He was the first person I'd ever lost," I said. "The only one, really. I never knew my dad's parents. And once Dad started going out of town on business a couple years earlier, Grandpa took up the slack. He was like my best friend. And when he died . . . well, there was only one person who could stop me from crying."

"Drew," she said. It wasn't a question.

I nodded.

"He came into my room," I recalled. "Didn't bother knocking. We never did. I was curled up in a ball on the bed. Sobbing. Holding on to Grandpa's fedora like it was him. Drew didn't know what to say. He just stayed with me. I think I sat up at some point. Must have." Some of the images from that day were still a bit blurry. "All I remember is him putting the fedora on my head. He leaned toward me when he did it. Kind of like how you're leaning in right now." This time there was no smack for my joke. "His lips were suddenly on mine. Kissing me. I was beyond surprised. Beyond shocked. I was thrilled. It felt so right. Before I knew it, I was kissing back. It felt so . . . comfortable. So nice."

I paused. Typically, Sam would tell me to hurry up and get to the rest, but she was savvy enough to know that the turn was coming.

"At about the time I finally relaxed," I continued, "Drew's eyes popped open. Even though he had started it—he had kissed me—he was in a panic. He may have said something to me. May have made some dumb excuse to explain what he was doing. A joke. I don't want to remember. All I know is, I blinked and he was gone. Out of my room. Out of my life."

"Wow" was all Sam could say.

Actually, she did say one other thing. "That might have something to do with why Hope and Drew broke up."

"Huh?"

"He was having intimacy issues," Sam said. "It was like he liked the idea of being a boyfriend more than he actually liked her. Not that he ever seemed all that interested in any other girls either. Hope had the distinct feeling that he just wasn't that into her. Maybe now we know why."

"When did . . . How . . . Why . . . We really need to share more!"

I'd spent all these years figuring it had been a one-time thing for Drew. Experimenting. Or that he didn't know what else to do with me crying there, so he did what he thought I wanted him to do. When he started dating Hope I just figured our encounter was all a mistake. A few times I'd convinced myself that I made it all up. But maybe there was something there. Because the way he'd left things with Hope gave me something I'd never had before . . .

Hope.

Gary gave the five-minute call, which meant it was time for the cast to get into places. My mind swimming, I wished them all to "break a leg" again and grabbed Hope's hand. We all left the green room together. I was confused but feeling a ton lighter for getting that off my chest . . . and only slightly guilty for throwing it at Sam right before she was about to go onstage.

As we parted, with Hope and me heading one way and the cast another, Sam had one last thing she wanted to do. "Hey, Bryan!"

I turned back just in time to see her lift her shirt and flash me like she did the one time she'd actually managed to screw me up before my entrance in our first production together.

This time? I was pretty unfazed by it. But Jason may have made a tiny slip out of character.

All's Well That Ends Well

What can be said about the performance? Well, a lot of things could be said and a lot of things were. The reviews were in and the critics were wowed!

"Bryan, that was wonderful," Mom said, and Dad added, "Just wonderful."

"Damn, that was fierce," Grandma said, and Blaine repeated, "Fierce!"

Mr. Randall called the play "A triumph."

Ms. Monroe thought it was "Spectacular."

Headmaster Collins went on to say, "It was a fine example of student productivity here at Orion Academy, where we do all that we can and must to showcase our fine learners in a practical setting, giving these young minds the chance to grow and explode with creativity."

Okay, ew . . . and huh?

It was the haters that gave us the most love.

"Not horrible," Holly said.

"Belle saved that show," Alexis added.

But the most important quote came from the most unlikely source as Jimmy Wilkey shooed us stragglers out of Hall Hall by shouting, "Time to party!"

The stunned silence that comment brought was followed by a huge burst of laughter, which was then broken up when Hope belted out that Rosemary Clooney (George's aunt) classic, *"Come on-a my house, my house!"* She led a parade of cast, crew, and parents out of the building and into the brisk air. It was a beautiful night for a party. No. It was a beautiful night for a celebration.

As we got into our respective vehicles—me with my folks, everyone else with their own—the show replayed in the movie of my mind. From Belle's entrance with the calla lilies to the ending . . . well, *you know* . . . every moment was magical. Not a line was dropped. Not a stage direction forgotten. And with the audience there, loving it, each moment was heightened to even better than it had been during the dress rehearsal. Suze's costumes looked great, Alexis hadn't done any real damage to her sister's hair, and Drew's painting positively shined in the spotlight that we'd set up to give it more focus at key points in the play. I was so lost in the memory that I barely realized that we'd reached the multimillion-dollar manse that is Hope's home.

"Damn," Grandma said. "I forgot how big they grew houses here in Malibu." When not traveling the world, Grandma lived in Northern California, helping a friend run her family winery.

"Sometimes I think I'm in the wrong business," Dad said.

"Hey, the world needs vice presidents of global initiatives for human rights studies more than it needs entertainment lawyers," I reminded him. He responded with a hug, forgetting about the bruised shoulder.

What? You really thought I didn't know what my own father did for a living?

Just don't ask me to explain it. All I know is that his job did give me the chance to meet Bono once.

The party was already in full swing when we arrived. Sam and Hope were waiting out front for me. We all entered to a chorus of cheers and well-wishing. And that was just the parents. The kids' party was relegated to the west wing of the house.

Yes, there is a whole other wing to party in. I try not to make too big a deal out of the money Hope has, but her dad could totally take over Eric's dad's company if he wanted to. And so could Hope's mom, for that matter.

"Welcome to Casa Rivera," Hope's dad said. His wife, cult actress Kara Bow, was on his arm. His ex-wife was holding court on the far side of the room. "Adults to the right. Kiddies to the left."

Kiddies?

My friends and I naturally turned to the right to join our folks. Well . . . that's where the good champagne was. I strolled over to the bar, which is where all the teachers had collected. Can you blame them? Mr. Rivera was serving *Cristal*. The adults all turned a blind eye to the three of us reaching for champagne, though Mr. Randall and Ms. Monroe tipped their glasses in a salute to us. (*Aside:* Ms. Monroe was sipping sparkling water.)

Before we could move on to the kiddie party, Mr. Randall tapped me on my shoulder. "Can I speak with you for a second? Privately?"

"Sure," I said, with a shrug to my friends. I told them to go on without me. I couldn't imagine what our teacher had to say, since the show was over and all the work was done. But one can never hear too many compliments, so I went along willingly.

We found a quiet spot in the next room; the Rivera library. Some day, I hope I have a home with its own library. Rather than commenting on the house's opulence, Mr. Randall got right down to business. "I had a word with the headmaster after the show."

"There is no such thing as *a* word with the headmaster," I reminded him.

"True," he agreed. "But we did have a discussion. About you, in fact."

"How flattering." *I hope.*

"As you know, Ms. Monroe is with child."

"It isn't mine."

"Bryan," he said sternly. "It's time to be serious."

"Understood," I said with my serious face.

He rolled his eyes. "Anyway. She's going on maternity leave in the spring. And as you know, we're going to go back to the regular schedule of having two nights of shows for the Spring Theatrical Production. One starring the seniors and sophomores . . ."

"And one for the juniors and freshmen," I added, wondering why he was telling me something I already knew. To be clear for those of you not in the know, it's not two different shows, but two versions of the same show. So that more students get to be involved in the production. We didn't get to do two shows during the *Wizard* debacle the previous spring (long story), but we'd be going back to the usual schedule this year. Mr. Randall directs the seniors' show while Ms. Monroe . . .

Oh.

"I can tell by the expression on your face that you see where this is going," Mr. Randall said.

"No!" But I did.

"Bryan, Ms. Monroe and I have talked about it. And the headmaster has agreed. We would love for you to direct the junior/freshman production of the school show."

Wow. Just . . . wow!

Of course, I couldn't let it go that easily. "You mean I can't direct the senior/sophomore production."

"Don't push it," he said.

"Do I get to help pick the play?" I asked.

"That power went right to your head, didn't it?" he asked. "But it's already been picked. Don't tell your friends. And I mean it. No telling Sam and Hope until the formal announcement. We still haven't cleared the rights. But if all goes well, we'll be doing *Wicked* this year."

Fitting.

Mr. Randall and I shared a toast to our new directorial

partnership and then returned to the party so I could race out to tell my friends part of what had just occurred.

I got to the game room and realized that even though Hope and Belinda were the stars of the evening, Alexis's fingerprints were all over the party planning. From the glittery, sparkly decorations to the DJ spinning electronic pop dance hits I didn't even recognize, it was a sight to behold. This wasn't some small soiree for the cast and crew. The whole school had been invited for one big blowout.

I downed my champagne. Okay, more like took a sip from my champagne and made a sour face because of the taste, but that doesn't sound nearly as sophisticated. Then I went to find my friends. Knowing them, I bypassed the revelry and took it outside to the quieter area by the pool, which is where I found Hope, Suze, Gary, and Drew along with Eric and Sam in their traditional position wrapped up in each other's arms.

"Hail, hail," Sam said now that the gang was all here. "Guess what."

"What?"

"Drew sold his first painting," Hope jumped in. "He sold all his paintings."

I looked to Drew, who was shyly staring at his shoes. "How? Who?"

"Anthony Mayflower," Sam said with a laugh. "He wants to buy the whole collection. Calls it an investment because Drew's going to be big someday."

"Well, Holly's dad is good at finding musical acts," I said. "Who knew he had an eye for artists as well?"

As I congratulated Drew and discussed what he should charge for his paintings, I decided to put my own good news on the back burner. I'd already had enough focus for one night. Besides, the moment I revealed that I'd be directing the spring show, the gossip would make the party rounds in a shot. Seniors would be upset with me. Juniors would start making a play for lead roles. Although, as I filled an empty spot in the circle beside Gary, I thought I may have already found the male lead.

"Where's the rest of my cast?" I stupidly asked once the conversation lulled.

Most of the people around me were awkwardly glancing around, but Hope threw out her arm and pointed in the direction of the pool house, where Jason and Belle were busy making out in the shadows.

Success! My plan had worked.

Uh-oh.

"They've been going at it since we got here," Sam said.

"Sounds like someone's jealous," Eric said. I could tell he meant it as a joke. The problem was that Sam knew it too.

"Like you should talk about jealous!" she said, overreacting in a way that was very unlike her.

"I apologized!" he said, releasing her.

"Yeah," she said. "And then you sure got over it fast enough."

"So, wait," he said. "Are you mad at me for being jealous or for not being jealous?"

"Exactly!" Sam said. Which is why I'm glad I'm her best friend and not her boyfriend.

Unfortunately, the raised voices brought unwanted attention. Belle and Jason had stopped making out and were making their way over to us. I was worried about what could be said with Jason in the mix, but I didn't realize the real problem was coming from the opposite direction.

"Knock it off!" Alexis yelled. "You're ruining my party."

"*Your* party!" Hope screamed, spinning on her stepsister. "When the hell did this become your party? This was *my* show. *My* night. Just because your sister managed to scheme her way into the cast—"

Seeing the hurt look on Belle's face, I tried to step in. "Hope!"

"You stay out of this!"

Tried and failed.

While Hope railed at her stepsisters, Sam and Eric went back to their argument over who was jealous and who was not jealous, even though there was nothing to be jealous about. The tensions that had been simmering for the past three weeks exploded into a fight that I was relieved we had managed to hold off until after the show.

"Hey, was that a shooting star?" Gary asked, coming up with the lamest excuse for an exit ever. The quality of excuse didn't matter to me, though. I took it and ran.

"Maybe," I said. "Let's go see."

Gary and I left the screaming group and the poor innocent victims around them who weren't fast enough to come up with their own lame excuses. We passed all the gaping stares and moved farther away from the house. Out there on the grounds it was even harder to hear the pounding beat of the abusive music and the more abusive fighting.

I led Gary through a small collection of pine trees that Hope had shown me once a few years ago. There was a small clearing at the edge of the property that had a beautiful unobstructed view of the ocean. Hope usually went there when she wanted to be alone. I figured it was as good a place as any to do what I had to do.

Too bad it sent the wrong message.

Gary took in the romantic surroundings and turned to face me. "It is my job as a stage manager to insulate my director from any and all grief," he said. "And that lame excuse was officially my last act in the position. I am now no longer your associate stage manager, which I hope means I am now free to become something else."

I went through those mental calculations again. It was true. We were no longer working together. We were free to pursue whatever we wanted . . . at least until the spring show, when I'd have to cast him in the play. But that was months off. There was nothing to stop us. Gary was cute. He was funny. And most of all, he was interested. The only negative was that he was one year younger than me, but that wasn't actually a real reason. In fact, there wasn't a good reason at all for me not to lean in as well.

Except . . .

"I'm sorry," I said. "I like you. But I don't think I like you, like you."

Gary was crushed. Or, okay, he was mildly disappointed. But he held up like a trooper. "I get it," he said. "Hey, who was that cute guy you were hanging out with from the Renaissance Faire a couple months back? Is he single?" Yeah. He was a trooper all right. I filled Gary in on Sam's Gay Best Friend, Marq. Considering he lived in San Francisco, I didn't see much of a future for them.

"You want to go back and see if the fireworks have died down?" he asked.

"Nah," I said. "This night's already been so draining. I need some time before I have to deal with any of that again."

Gary nodded. "You wanna make out, just for the hell of it?"

Talk about breaking the tension. That was a needed laugh. "Tempting," I said, recovering. "But you should save your first kiss with a guy to be something special."

"Who said you'd be my first kiss?" he replied with an impish smile before disappearing back through the bushes.

Okay, when I turned down Sam's GBF, Marq, over the summer it was mainly because he wasn't my type. But Gary? He was exactly my type, if I even had such a thing. I could totally see myself in a relationship with him. And let's be honest, it's not like there were a lot of choices at Orion Academy. Granted, if you're going to like boys, it's much easier to do in the L.A. area than other parts of the world. But it all came down to me not wanting to settle. Not when I'd known what I wanted all along.

"Hey," Drew said, coming through the bushes. I couldn't have directed a more perfect cue. "Gary said you wanted to see me. And what, pray tell, was going on in this secluded corner of the party?"

Leave it to Gary to still be looking out for his director. "Not what *you're* thinking," I assured Drew.

"You broke his heart, didn't you?"

"I don't know about that," I said. "But I did let him down easy."

Drew nodded as if he understood.

"Because I'm in love with you," I added, to make it clear.

If you're reading this, thinking to yourself, "well, now, *that* came out rather suddenly," I assure you I was way more surprised I said it than you are. But no one was more surprised than Drew. And it wasn't all that sudden. It had been building since that day we first met. So long ago that neither of us actually remembered it.

Before Drew could say anything, I kissed him. I went right in, met his lips, and planted myself there for the duration. It wasn't passionate. It wasn't full of emotion like that first one years ago. It was tentative. It was awkward. It was just a simple kiss.

And it was perfect.

Because he kissed me back.

We stayed locked together, letting the kiss grow and become something less simple. We both knew that things had been leading here for the longest time. There was so much we had to say. So much to talk about. To deal with. But that was for some other time. For now we wanted to live in the moment. Not to say that I couldn't have some fun with him.

I held up my arm and pointedly checked my watch out of the corner of my eye.

"Got somewhere to be?" he asked, his lips still pressed to mine.

"Just timing you," I said. "Seeing how long before you run."

He ended the kiss with a smile. "You're an ass."

"So I've been told."

And then he took my hand and walked me back to the party.

You're a Good Man, Charlie Brown

I guess Hope's dad had said something about the noise from the "kiddie party" because the DJ had turned down the music so much that we couldn't even hear it out by the pool. It's a good thing too, because once Drew and I stepped out of the bushes, hand in hand, the music probably would have stopped dead. Like the conversation did.

It was a brief pause, dotting through the crowd. And then a buzz about something new rippled after it. The latest gossip to make the rounds. Then the conversations resumed at regular volume and life went back to normal.

Even when I'm being scandalous, I don't cause much of a scandal.

We rejoined our group, where things were much calmer than they'd been when I'd left. Eric had his arms around Sam again. Hope was actually standing beside Belle, willingly. Suze and Jason were also there, but Gary was inside the game room with his best friend, Madison. She was glaring at me through the window and probably trash-talking as a best friend is supposed to do.

Holly and Alexis? Nowhere to be seen.

I checked the pool for bodies, but it was clear.

Meanwhile, Hope and Sam were giving me looks—well, I was afraid their eyes were going to pop out and fall into the pool. Eric's eyes were locked on the hand-holding and he had a stupid grin on his face. Then he gave us both a nod that I took to mean "It's about damn time."

Nobody said anything, though we were all dying to.

"Okay," I said to Drew, breaking the tension. I pointed to Sam and Hope with my free hand. "They need to talk to me before they explode. And I'm pretty sure Eric wants to talk to you too."

"Doubtless," Drew replied.

"Why don't we split up and reconvene in a few minutes," I suggested.

"I like that plan," he said.

We both moved in like we were going to kiss good-bye, but stopped ourselves. Neither of us was quite there for PDAs yet, but give us time.

I reluctantly let go of Drew's hand. Before I could even miss it, Sam's hand had taken its place. And Hope had grabbed my other one. They pulled me off, past the pool house to the side of the property where Hope had insisted her dad keep her dog's house even though Daisy had died years ago. The house was so big the three of us could sit in it, and it was designed in the spitting image of Snoopy's doghouse from the *Peanuts* comics. It was another one of the many places on the property Hope liked to go to be alone.

"Spill!" they said in unison once we were safely inside the makeshift clubhouse. And spill I did. I told them everything. The things they already knew. The things they never guessed. I admitted things to them that I'd never admitted to myself.

Not a single one of those things came as a surprise to any of us.

"Does this mean we can double-date?" Sam asked.

And, for a change, I smacked her. Only lightly. And on the arm. But it felt good.

"I guess that depends on if you and Eric are still together," I said.

"We are," she said. "We were both just being stupid."

"Both?"

"Well, maybe me a bit more," she said. "Just a bit!"

"And those feelings you were having for Jason?"

"Ha!" Hope burst out, as if she knew something I didn't.

Sam glared at her. "Turns out you guys were right. It was the character, not me. As soon as we had the curtain call, all those confusing feelings I was having totally disappeared."

I shook my head. Actors are truly, truly insane.

"All that drama," I said. "Over nothing."

"Isn't that what all good drama turns out to be about in the end?" Hope asked.

We all nodded together as if nothing more needed to be said.

I leaned back against the wall of the late Daisy's doghouse. The night's drama was over, but I suspected that all new kinds of drama weren't far off. In a few months we'd start preparing for the Spring Theatrical Production, which no doubt would be rife with even more insanity. Since I'd be directing the junior/freshman production, it would be weird not working with my friends this time. But I wouldn't be able to keep them away from those rehearsals.

Maybe it was time to accept that I was now a full-fledged director, with one whole production under my belt and everything. I kind of like the sound of director-photographer. Not that I've had the time to take many pictures lately. I've been too busy trying to figure out who I am, like everyone else I know.

The truth is, it changes every day. Titles don't really mean anything, no matter how many hyphens you have. Then again, I kind of like the one I ultimately came up with for myself. I am now a director-photographer–former actor–doggie design store second assistant manager–student–son–fedoraless grandson–best friend–possible boyfriend . . .

An octuple hyphenate.

With room to grow.

About the Author

Paul Ruditis first set foot onstage in the second grade when he appeared as a space alien in a play about finding the true meaning of Christmas. He's also worked on plays about comic-strip characters, a teen pop star, a man-eating plant, space pandas, singing gangsters, clowns, rogue cows, and Hell. His diverse theatrical training has served him well in writing the DRAMA! series.

Find out more at www.paulruditis.com.

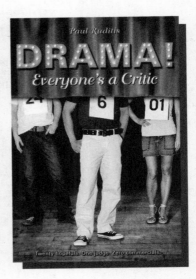

Let's get this straight . . .

Jonathan Parish is seventeen, out and proud—and accidentally winds up in bed with a *girl*? Yup—an inebriated lapse of judgment leads him to sleep with a member of his angsty-straight-girl posse at a party. Word soon gets around that hot-but-previously-unavailable Jonathan might be on the market. And his school's It girl makes him a proposition: if he pretends to be her boyfriend, she'll fly him to London to attend a Kylie Minogue concert.

With his eye on the prize, Jonathan will do pretty much anything to see his beloved pop star Kylie up close and personal. Even if it means acting like he's straight and going back into the closet. . . .

the straight road to Kylie

nico Medina

"I can't get this book outta my head."
—RACHEL COHN,
bestselling author of *Gingerbread*

From **Simon Pulse**
Published by Simon & Schuster